Hot Pursuit

Madalyn's breathing grew labored and perspiration broke out on her forehead and between her breasts. Ice-cold terror set in anew. She couldn't believe this was happening. From Hollywood darling to dead woman in the blink of an eye.

She could hear the crunch of heavy boots on the snow growing closer; she could all but feel the hot breath of her pursuer on her neck. He was only about four giant steps from reaching her.

"*Noooo!*" she cried out as his rough hands seized her hips from behind. She screamed as she fell to the ground, his heavy body coming down hard on top of hers.

"You are fine," a deep, heavily accented voice murmured to Madalyn. "Be still."

Sweet God, she had never been so frightened. Black eyes locked with scared green ones. She felt this close to passing out.

"What do you want?" she asked, her voice catching.

"I want you."

This title is also available as an eBook

ALSO BY JAID BLACK

Tie Me Up, Tie Me Down
by Sherrilyn Kenyon
Melanie George
Jaid Black

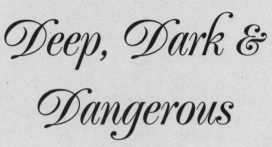

Deep, Dark & Dangerous

JAID BLACK

POCKET BOOKS
New York   London   Toronto   Sydney

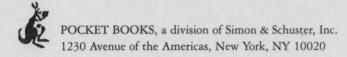

POCKET BOOKS, a division of Simon & Schuster, Inc.
1230 Avenue of the Americas, New York, NY 10020

ISBN-13: 978-1-4165-1612-5
ISBN-10:   1-4165-1612-3

First Pocket Books trade paperback edition March 2006

10 9 8 7 6 5 4 3 2 1

Manufactured in the United States of America

For information regarding special discounts for bulk purchases, please contact Simon & Schuster Special Sales at 1-800-456-6798 or business@simonandschuster.com

To my agent, Ethan Ellenberg, for putting up with me. To my editor at Pocket Books, Micki Nuding, for her unwavering enthusiasm and keen editorial eye. And to Napoleon and Vinny for greeting me every morning with excited pants, slobbery kisses, and wagging tails. (Now if only I could get my husband to do that . . .)

Prologue

Verily, a time of great suffering shall fall upon the whole of the world, for its women will dwindle in numbers. Disease shall soon spread, female babes will not be born, and bloodliness will die out. But, yea, the strong Vikings shall live on, for almighty Odin has seen fit to warn us. We are His chosen people.

Take to the earth, the haven bequeathed to us; the belly of the gods. Dwell below her dirt and leaves, now and forever, untouched by the Outsiders and their ways.

Yea, let each warrior cling unto a wife, that his seed may bear fruit and our race prevail. Should a time come when there are fewer females than warriors in our stronghold, then hunt on the Outside and take them.

By any means necessary, take them.

—Viking legend

Otar Thordsson absently stared at the words on the seven-hundred-year-old statue. Like his people, the carved image of Erikk the Mighty, his great-grandfather many generations removed, had endured through the passage of time. Both were built from the same unyielding grit and mettle.

Lost in thought, Otar stared at the statue. A grim frown shadowed Otar's features.

The Revolution was coming. Soon, the time would be upon the warriors of New Sweden to seize back the kingdom and place it in the hands of the jarl who was meant to rule it—Nikolas Ericsson.

The Thordssons had lost much under Toki's regime, the current jarl-king. Once of the ruling class of nobles, his family had been sentenced to toil amongst the laborers.

A cousin to Toki, Otar hadn't been shocked when the inevitable came to pass. Toki could stomach no threat to his reign; he retained his position by snuffing out any potential blood rivals to the kingship. Or so he believed . . .

Otar ran a hand over his plaited back raven hair. In truth, he had posed less of a threat to Toki amongst the soft nobility. Now, a decade later, his six-foot-six-inch frame was not gangly and thinly postured, but powerful, honed, and heavily muscled.

Perfect for snapping Toki's twiggy neck with his callused hands.

Otar didn't wish to retain the kingship for himself. Truth be told, he'd rather remain amongst the laborers than endure such a headache. Leastways Toki's sire had wished Lord Nikolas Ericsson to rule the Underground kingdom of New Sweden upon his death, and so it would be.

Otar picked up his hammer and headed toward the grindstone. There was a lot of work to be done, pounding metals into goods that could be bartered amongst the other Underground clans of New Norway and New Daneland for more weapons.

Now was the time for laboring. Soon it would be time for the Revolution. It had to be so. There was more at stake than a personal vendetta.

Someday, when the prophecies came to pass, it was imperative that their people be led through tumultuous times with a strong hand and keen mind. Toki could not and would not ever be that man. Under his regime, their race would die out.

Under Nikolas's rule, the Vikings would thrive, and once again their people would rule the whole of the world.

Chapter One

"*Why hast thou forsaken me?*" she raged to the heavens. "*Why? Oh God . . . why?!*" She shook as she turned away from Alejandro's bulging biceps. She felt his heated stare searing her back with its intensity. "*I cannot bear this temptation another minute, Lord. I cannot!*"

Alejandro's nostrils flared as he turned her in his embrace. "*You will make love with me, Sister Alexis.*" He shook her as she cried out for mercy. "*You are mine.*"

"*Noooooo!*"

"Leave the church, my beloved." His voice was low and insistent, his breathing heavy. "Let us consummate our love."

"Never," she gasped, backing away from him.

Sister Alexis tightly clutched the rosary beads she held, wielding them like a talisman. Her eyes were drawn to his bare washboard stomach and the beads fell to the ground, forgotten.

"No!" she protested, even as she threw herself in Alejandro's awaiting arms. He wildly kissed her as he ripped at her nunnery clothes. "Nooooooo!"

Thirty-year-old Madalyn Simon frowned up at the movie screen. Sweet Lord above, what had she been drinking when she agreed to play the role of a cloistered nun who fell in love with a matador? There were low points in an actress's life and then there were *low* points. This farce was a bottomless pit of lowness.

"I have fought the horns of many deadly bulls," Alejandro purred, "but never have I been caught by them until you, Sister Alexis."

Madalyn winced. How bad would it look if she walked out on the premiere of her own movie? Her agent would maim her. Her manager would kill what was left of her after the maiming.

"I have prayed for many souls," Sister Alexis gasped as she stroked Alejandro's hard belly, "yet I never really understood what having a soul meant until I locked eyes with you."

But then, her agent and manager didn't have to see themselves dressed like a nun in the arms of a shirtless Spanish matador muttering some of the dumbest lines ever put to paper.

She sighed. She really had to quit making movie deals over nachos and piña coladas.

"Take me, Alejandro! Show me what it means to be a woman!"

That's it! She no longer cared what anyone thought. She wasn't going to watch herself look foolish for another second. There were still thirty torturous minutes left to endure until *The Taming of the Shrewd* was over; the rest of the crew could endure those minutes without her.

Delicately clearing her throat, she smoothed the French twist her golden-red hair had been fashioned into as she stood up. If there was ever a perfect moment to suck down a piña colada, this was it.

"Where are you going?" her manager whispered through a tight-lipped smile from beside her. He tugged at her arm.

"I need some air."

"You can't walk out now," he whined.

"I can and I am."

His dark eyes looked desperate. "The studio won't take kindly to this."

"Bruno—"

"Sit!" he barked under his breath.

"You sit!" Madalyn hissed back.

If she didn't leave now, it would be even more difficult to skip the after-premiere party, and there was no way in heaven or hell she was showing up for *that*.

Oh yes, the "glorious" after-premiere party! Jealous actresses lying through their teeth about how fabulous *The Taming of the Shrewd* was, while secretly gloating that

America's beloved Madalyn Simon was going downhill. Wannabe actresses doing the same thing, but for the purpose of getting in her good graces instead of disparaging her. Bruno looking scared that he'd have to settle for ten million instead of twenty million for Madalyn's next movie. The studio executives whispering to each other about what to do for damage control . . .

Where had it all gone wrong? Madalyn wondered not for the first time. In the beginning, she had picked roles with the panache and eye of a high-stakes gambler in Monte Carlo. These days she picked them like a has-been at the bingo hall back in her hometown of Athens, Alabama.

Because you no longer care.

Madalyn briefly closed her catlike green eyes and sighed. It was true. She really didn't care anymore.

Hollywood had turned out to be the very epitome of glitzy superficiality it was touted as. Nobody could be taken at face value, everyone wanted something from you, divorces could be ordered up quicker than a stiff drink, and lies were as commonplace as the L.A. smog.

During the past decade she had seen countless actors and actresses give in to the dark side of the force, becoming as jaded and artificial as legend bespoke. Madalyn, on the contrary, never had.

At heart, Madalyn Mae Simon was an Alabama girl in a Barbie world. Given to being something of a drama queen, she wasn't perfect by any stretch of the imagination, but she was decent and kind inside. She wanted things to stay that way.

Her heartbeat picking up in tempo, Madalyn yanked her porcelain-colored arm out of Bruno's meaty, tanning bed–bronzed hand.

"I'm leaving," she said definitively. She felt like the exorcist, battling Bruno for the possession of her soul. Yeah, she was a drama queen. Oh well. "Unless you want a scene, respect that."

Shocked gazes followed her as she made her way to the back of the theater. Picking up the hem of her dress, Madalyn notched her chin up, waved to her limo driver, and regally left the building. The perfect exit. At least she could still do those with gusto.

Her shoulders slumped as soon as the limo doors were safely shut behind her. Sweet Lord above, she needed that piña colada.

"YES, I REALLY AM DOING IT, DRAKE. I'm leaving Hollywood behind for good and moving someplace where nobody knows me. Quit laughing!"

"I'm trying," her sister chuckled. "Really."

"Uh-huh. I can hear that."

"Oh come on, Maddie Mae, do you know how many times you've said this very same thing to me?"

Madalyn sniffed. "I don't remember—"

"I do. Twenty."

"And *don't* call me Maddie Mae." Her lips pinched together. "It makes me sound like I live in a trailer with ten kids and a potbellied husband named Earl.

"Listen," Madalyn said, haphazardly throwing clothes into suitcases. The cordless phone was perched between her ear and shoulder. "I'm serious this time, Drake. I'm packing as we speak."

Her sister chuckled. "And do you remember how many times you've packed your suitcases only to unpack them an hour later?"

"Not really," she ground out.

"I do. Twenty."

"You're starting to irritate me. Why do I even bother to call you for support?"

"Because I'm your sister and I love you. And by the way, guess how many times you've said *that* to me?"

"Twenty?"

"Nope. Thirty-five."

Madalyn's shoulders slumped. She couldn't deny what her younger sister said. She had, in fact, done all those things, perhaps even more often than Drake had counted. And yet . . .

Deep down inside, Madalyn knew that this time was different. This time she meant it. Perhaps turning thirty last week had indelibly changed something. Realizing that she was a thirty-year-old woman with piles of money, no family save Drake, and no real friends, had been jarring.

It had changed everything.

The desire to bolt from Hollywood was as all-consuming now as it had been several hours back when she'd left Bruno and the movie showing behind. Usually she calmed down an hour or so later, telling herself things would get better—but they never did. She didn't aspire to money and a career—she had those things already. What kept her going all these years were dreams of making real friends, finding a loyal, trustworthy mate, and . . .

Her nostrils flared. It didn't matter. They were all illusions. In this superficial world, they would *always* be illusions.

"If you're serious this time," Drake said after a long pause, "you know you're always welcome to live with me."

Madalyn tried not to snort. "Yeah, I can already see the headlines: 'Madalyn Simon Gives Up on Life After the Humiliating Flop *The Taming of the Shrewd* and Flees to Utah to Live with Alarmist, Antigovernment Sister." She sighed. "I appreciate the offer, but I want to go where I can't be found. As soon as I leave Hollywood, the first place the reporters will flock to is your head-for-the-hills barricade outside Salt Lake City."

"Don't knock it. The facility we've set up here is primo. Once chemical warfare commences, we'll be the only human survivors. And, oh yes, war *will* happen soon. Did you read in the paper about . . ."

Madalyn plopped down on her Arabian princess haremesque bed, tucked a stray curl behind one ear, and smiled into the phone. She and Drake couldn't be more different if they tried, but she loved her little sister fiercely. More than once, she'd chewed out a reporter for making fun of Drake's beliefs and lifestyle in the paper. Nobody, but nobody, said anything negative about Drake Simon and got away with it. Not if Madalyn had something to say about it.

Drake and Madalyn: no two blood sisters could be less alike. The only things they shared in common were green eyes and five-foot-eight-inch frames. There the similarities ended. Madalyn favored their mother with her ivory skin and long, curly, golden red hair. Drake took after their father, with long, straight, inky black hair and skin that tanned easily. After both of their parents died, Madalyn made a permanent move to California. Drake took off with her the-sky-is-falling-and-the-government-cannot-be-trusted friends and headed for an underground barricade in Utah.

Madalyn lay back on her bed and patiently waited for her sister's political rant to come to an end. When Drake was through pontificating on how the CACW—Citizens Against Chemical Warfare—were certain that the United States government was experimenting on alien corpses, Madalyn interjected.

"I'm serious this time. I really am leaving, Drake."

Silence.

"Where will you go? I doubt there's any place left on earth where people won't recognize you."

Unfortunately, Drake was probably right. "I don't know, sis," Madalyn sighed, "but I'm going to find it."

Chapter Two

Arctic Seacoast
Two Months Later

Madalyn *fell onto her bed* with a happy sigh. She was probably the only person in harsh, rural Alaska with a seventy-thousand-dollar bed that looked like it belonged to a sultan's favored 'harem' girl, but oh well. There were some things she'd been willing to part with when she secretly sold off her estate, and some things she hadn't been willing to give up. Her beloved bed had been one of the latter.

"I can't believe I did it," she told the log cabin walls with a smile. "But I did."

The papers and TV were abuzz with reports of Madalyn

Simon's disappearance—or so Drake had told her via the phone. Newspapers were scarce out in the Arctic and television sets were even rarer, so all her reports came second-hand.

Madalyn's closest neighbors were a nearby village of Eskimos. Nice people, and thankfully they spoke enough English to communicate with her, but they didn't have a clue as to who she was. Perfect!

Every few days Madalyn would don one of her en vogue ski suits and drive her expensive snowmobile into the Inuit tribe's village to buy the necessary survival supplies. She enjoyed the trips, mostly because they gave her a reason to be around other people.

When she'd dreamt of chucking it all and leaving civilization behind, she hadn't realized how lonely life would be. It was a solitary life out here, but still far superior to her old, emotionally devoid one.

Madalyn turned over on her belly, propped her hands beneath her chin, and sighed. As much as she was enjoying this sojourn from reality, she didn't know how much longer she could withstand it. Life out here was more demanding than she'd realized—especially for a woman who hadn't cooked a meal, made a bed, or done her own cleaning in over fifteen years. She had assumed it would all come back to her, sort of like riding a bicycle. She had assumed wrong.

Every time she chipped a nail, she dropped everything until it was once again neatly manicured. Whenever she was attempting to clean her log cabin and dust got into her nose, she sneezed for a solid ten minutes. Madalyn grimly wondered just how badly *it* had gotten to her.

It—Hollywood. Had the Alabama girl become part of the Barbie world without even realizing her soul had been lost? Lord, she needed an exorcism! *And* a piña colada. Bartered goat milk was getting a little boring.

The phone rang, jarring Madalyn out of her self-pitying reverie. Drake! Her sister was the only person who knew how to reach her.

Scampering off her bed, Madalyn ran toward the kitchen for the high-tech CACW-issued mobile phone her sister had given her. She cursed under her breath as she fumbled with the metal gadget, trying to remember the code that would permit her to open it. If she entered the wrong password, the thing would explode in her hand.

"Shit!" she screeched, unable to recall the elaborate code. Why Drake had made the numeric sequence so long was beyond her. On a good day, Madalyn could barely recall the four-digit security code to her old mansion.

The phone stopped ringing. Defeated, Madalyn sighed. When she threw the piece of metal down on the kitchen counter, she noticed a tiny screen for text messaging that she hadn't noticed before. Her eyes narrowed as she read the words that flowed over the pixilated screen:

Your password is 5789127, 687775214, 8, 1111878835, 9856327, 87458758524632, 8747, 89895642, 87458, 7, 568975418, 58741. This time write it down.

She frowned, then picked up a pen and scribbled down

the outrageous password. How could anyone memorize something so ridiculously long?

When the phone rang again, Madalyn was prepared. Biting her tongue in concentration—a childhood habit she'd never been able to shed—she punched in the proper sequence. She smiled with accomplishment when she opened the phone without her hand and half her head getting blown off.

"It's wonderful to hear your voice, Drake. I miss you!"

"I miss you, too, Maddie Mae."

Madalyn was so overjoyed to talk to her sister that she let the "Maddie Mae" go unpunished. "How have you been? When are you coming to see me? Are you—"

Drake whistled. "Whoa! One question at a time. I've been okay, but I doubt I'll be seeing you anytime soon. The vultures are still swarming and Big Brother is hot on my case."

Madalyn understood Drake's vocabulary with nary a pause. Vultures were reporters and Big Brother was government police of some sort. Why wouldn't they just leave Drake alone? Didn't they understand that Madalyn didn't want to be found? She'd assumed the letter she'd left behind with a lawyer would explain everything.

"I see," Madalyn said, her good mood deflating. She should have become a waitress rather than an actress. Then she could disappear without the bounty on her head being so high.

"Hey, sis . . . you okay?"

"Not really."

Madalyn sighed, telling Drake how lonely and difficult life was turning out to be in rugged Alaska. She loved the solitude and the genuineness of the few people she'd met, but she wasn't as self-sufficient as she'd believed herself to be. Life was hard. Being alone so much was even harder.

"As much as I hate admitting to it, Drake, I just don't know if I'm cut out for this. I'm as soft as people say. I didn't want to believe it, but it's true."

"Oh, bullshit."

One of Madalyn's eyebrows inched up. "Eh?"

"I said 'bullshit.' You, Maddie Mae, are one of the toughest people, male or female, I've ever met. Even in Hollywood, and you've always been outspoken when you believed in something—even if it could have cost you your career. You don't take crap from anyone. And whenever you set your mind to do something, by God, you do it."

Madalyn was so taken aback by her sister's praise that it took a moment to recover. Drake never gushed like that. She felt an emotional lump the size of an apple form in her throat. "Th-thank you." She swallowed a bit roughly. "That's the most wonderful thing anyone has ever said to me."

"Well, it's true. The problem is, you haven't yet made up your mind to see this Alaskan thing through. Once you do, I know you'll come out on top. You always do."

Her spine straightened at the compliment. It was just the boost her ego needed. "Thank you, Drake."

"No thanks are necessary."

"I'm going to do it," Madalyn said firmly, her chin notching up. "I will learn to take care of myself in Alaska if it's the last thing I ever do!"

"That a girl!"

Madalyn shook her head up and down as though Drake could see her. "I will learn to cook, clean, and defend myself."

"Go get 'em!"

She waved a hand regally through the air. "I will learn to sew—well, probably not," she amended, "but I *will* learn how to milk that damn goat I bought."

"I believe you."

"If the mountain won't come to Mohammed, then Mohammed will go to the mountain!" Madalyn wasn't precisely certain what that meant, but it added flair to the significant moment.

"That's the CACW motto."

By the time their phone call ended, Madalyn had vowed that she would stay in Alaska if it killed her. Blowing out a breath as she closed the mobile and peered outside the window at her goat, she decided that it just might.

OTAR THORDSSON SMILED at the beautiful wench on screen as he sipped from a tankard of ale. He'd only seen a handful of moving pictures in his lifetime, but this one was his favorite.

The saga was about an English girl with hair of golden red who resisted the wooing of a dark, formidable Viking who had conquered her family's stronghold. 'Twas a ridiculous flight of fancy, yet Otar enjoyed the movie immensely.

All Outsider contraptions were illegal in the Underground, but Lord Ericsson occasionally showed movies in secret to a select few he trusted after the working day was done. This eve was such an occasion. With the men preparing for the war that would either reclaim New Sweden or cost them their lives—or both—they needed a harmless way to blow off a little steam.

"I love this part," an older warrior named Otrygg mused. He waggled his eyebrows and rubbed his callused palms together. "'Tis time for the Viking lord to claim the wench that belongs to him."

That announcement met with a few chuckles. Indeed, this was Otar's favored part of the picture as well. How could it not be? The tiny lass with the golden-red hair was preparing to remove her dress and show off her naked bosom.

Later, when the moving picture was over, Otar knew he'd soon be doing one of two things—pounding into the body of a willing widow or pumping his own shaft like a man possessed. Either way, 'twould be thoughts of the wench on the screen that consumed him. It was always the way of it.

The warriors ceased their prattling as the gorgeous girl's dress was peeled off her body. Otar's cock stirred in his leather braes at the sight of those deliciously erect nipples. 'Twas amazing. He'd seen this particular movie, *Song of the*

Viking, a score of times, yet he never failed to get hard each and every time those pink nipples popped up on the screen.

Otar's dark gaze narrowed, his eyelids heavy with arousal. Sweet Odin, how he wanted that wench. If he knew where to find her, he'd steal her in a heartbeat.

"I'm afraid the moving picture ends here for the eve," Lord Ericsson announced as he entered the dark, earthen chamber. "There is trouble brewing."

Otar looked quizzically to Otrygg, who shrugged in ignorance. One black eyebrow inched up as Otar turned to regard his cousin. "What has happened, Nikolas?"

"'Tis Toki." Lord Ericsson's jaw tightened. "The fool was spotted above the ground. Worse yet, I believe he was seen by the Outsider warriors."

Otar stilled. "Which ones?" he asked softly.

Nikolas sighed. "The ones that call themselves 'Army.'"

"Fuck."

"My thoughts exactly."

This was not good. Otar had spied on the warriors of Army on more than one occasion, and they knew what they were about. If Toki's presence had drawn their curiosity, it could spell trouble for all the clans of the three Underground kingdoms. None could know of their existence. Not for many, many more years to come.

"Otar!" Nikolas barked.

Otar stood up and inclined his head. He would do whatever was asked of him and every man present knew it. "Aye, milord?"

Similar in height, the two raven-haired men easily locked eyes. "You know what needs to be done," Nikolas said.

"I do." He would hunt, spy, and—should the situation warrant it—kill.

Lord Ericsson inclined his head. "Go do it."

Chapter Three

Madalyn hummed a favorite show tune—the only show tune she knew, actually—as she pulled a loaf of homemade bread out of the oven. She paused humming long enough to inhale the fresh, heavenly scent. She hoped it would taste as delicious as it smelled.

"Good grief," a perplexed voice said, startling a yelp out of her. "What happened here? Did Big Brother take over your body or something?"

Madalyn whirled around. "Drake," she breathed out, her heart drumming like mad from the fright she'd been given.

Drake winked. "I knew you would learn how to take

care of yourself, Maddie Mae. I didn't know you'd turn into Betty Crocker."

The old Madalyn would have been insulted by such a comment. Apparently the new Madalyn was, too. "I'm not Betty Crocker. And for the love of God, please quit calling me Maddie Mae!"

Within seconds, Madalyn's glower kicked up into a smile. "You're really here?" she whispered. "I'm not having some sort of goat milk–induced hallucination?"

"It's possible you're hallucinating," Drake said seriously. "Do you know what kind of chemicals the government feeds to farm animals? Just yesterday I read about—"

"Oh, shut up and hug me already!" Madalyn laughed. She grinned like an idiot as she ran across the floor and threw her arms around her little sister. "Goodness, Drake, I've missed you! Please tell me you'll be staying a while?"

Drake hugged her back, the love she felt for Madalyn clear in her embrace. "Of course." Glancing around the cabin, her smile faded. "I need to fortify this puppy a bit better."

Madalyn was too overjoyed by Drake's announcement that she planned to stay a while to give her alarmist comment much thought. Besides, that was just Drake, and she accepted her sister for who she was.

"Would you like a tour of the cabin first?" Madalyn asked. "Sounds good."

DRAKE HAD BEEN RIGHT, Madalyn thought with a feeling of accomplishment. Once she made up her mind to do something, she did it, come hell or high water. She had learned to cook for herself and clean the log cabin without breaking into sneezing fits. She was becoming a better barterer at the Inuit trading village. Hell, she was even teaching herself a few self-defense techniques she'd gleaned from one of those boring CACW manuals her sister had given her before she'd left for Alaska.

The one thing Madalyn hadn't tried to do yet was milk her goat, Victoria. Now that Drake was here, she would have to. It was either that or buy a ton of milk from the nearby village.

"Are you sure you can do it by yourself?" Drake asked skeptically.

Madalyn nodded as she neared her goat. "Victoria seems to like me. I'm sure it'll be okay."

"Victoria? You named a goat Victoria?"

"If you bothered to watch any of my movies, you'd know it was the name of the very first leading lady I ever played."

"*Song of the Viking.*" Drake nodded. "I saw it. Been trying to block the visual of what your tits look like from my memory ever since."

Madalyn ignored that. Plopping a pail on the ground next to Victoria, she concentrated on the task at hand. "Okay," she said, unsure of herself, "here goes nothing."

"Um, Maddie Mae . . ."

"Shhh! I'm about to touch her, uh, boobie. Don't frighten her."

"Don't touch that!"

Madalyn glanced up, the alarm in her sister's voice breaking her concentration. "What is the problem?" She rolled her eyes. "Don't tell me that nature girl can't stand to watch a goat get milked."

Drake frowned. "I'd gladly watch what you so scientifically referred to as a 'boobie' get milked, but that ain't no boobie. And I'm guessing Victoria should have been named Victor."

Madalyn's green eyes widened. "You mean . . . ?"

Drake nodded. "Afraid so. I don't think I want to drink anything that comes out of that thing."

"How gross!"

"I'm with you on that one."

Angry, Madalyn shot up to her feet. "That damn man who sold me Victoria promised me she was a girl! I decided to buy her even though she only had one boobie because I felt sorry for her. That snake-oil salesman told me she'd had a partial mastectomy!"

Drake sighed. "Have you ever heard of a goat getting a mastectomy?"

Madalyn threw her hands up in the air. "What do I know about goats? Damn him! I'm just grateful I got tired last night and decided not to milk her—him—as originally planned."

Drake winced.

"I guess we'll have to go into the village to buy milk." Madalyn sighed. "Sorry, sis."

"Hey, as long as you're sure it's really milk they're selling, I don't mind."

"Good grief, I hope so."

"I'm sure it is." Drake inclined her head toward Victoria. "We can try to find that goat trader, too, and make him exchange him."

Madalyn's eyes rounded. "No way! I can't give Victoria away just because she is a he." She petted the goat and smiled. "It follows me everywhere. I rather like him. We'll have to buy another goat."

"Fine. Just let me do the talking this time. And remember something."

"What?"

"Boobies always come in pairs."

"Right."

OTAR GAVE THE SIGNAL for the two warriors he'd chosen to accompany him on the mission to approach the hidden door that led to the Outside. Having already checked for invaders, he knew none were about.

All three men were dressed in the way of their people—leather braes and boots, sleeveless tunics, and bangles clasped about their biceps. For camouflage they wore polar bear skins—heavy white furs that kept them warm whilst shielding others from being aware of their presence.

Otar looked at his approaching men. Luukas was considered to be a bit touched in the head by their people, but he was a talented ferreter of information and people nonetheless. Iiro didn't share Luukas's insane bloodlust, but a finer hunter didn't exist.

"'Tis time," he told them. "Let us do this now and do it quickly."

"YOU'RE WEARING *THAT?*" Drake asked.

Madalyn's forehead wrinkled as she gazed into her sister's green eyes that were dead ringers for her own. Frowning, she smoothed out her ski suit with her hands. "Did I sit in coffee or something?" she asked, twisting her head back and forth to try to get a look at her rear end.

"No, you didn't sit in anything. Maddie Mae—"

"I really wish you wouldn't call me that!"

"Come here. Stand in front of the mirror and let's inspect that thing you call an outfit versus what I'm wearing."

"I'll have you know that this is a Christian Dior design," Madalyn sniffed. "It's gorgeous."

"It's pink."

"Pink and gorgeous."

Drake looked like she wanted to hit somebody. Namely Madalyn. "Come here," she said again, tugging at her sister's arm. "Stand in front of the mirror and tell me what you see."

Madalyn followed her sister's lead. Gazing in the mirror, she gave herself the once-over: Pink ski suit trimmed with faux pink fur. Matching pink boots. Long, honey-red curls wound into a knot before flowing down her back. Pink sunglasses garnished with diamonds.

Madalyn shrugged. "This outfit is great. I think it's very pretty."

"Pretty in Hollyweird," Drake said pointedly.

Madalyn stilled. The light came on. "Oh good grief, I'm an idiot," she muttered.

"No you're not," Drake promised, patting her on the back. "You just aren't accustomed to survivalist living yet." She nodded with an air of authority. "Luckily for you and your desire to not be recognized, I am."

"Great." Madalyn sighed, looking at her sister's polar-bear-skin-over-khaki outfit like a deer caught in headlights. "I can hardly wait to see what kind of outfit you put me in."

Chapter Four

The village of Zhitana was so tiny, remote, and unknown that it wasn't even found on any Alaskan maps, let alone in United States atlases.

"You look great!" Drake yelled, so she'd be heard above the snowmobile's loud engine. "Don't worry so much!"

Madalyn thought she looked like a militant psychopath who'd recently fought a polar bear to the death, but she supposed it didn't matter. The point was to not stick out in a crowd. The fact that she wasn't an Inuit was already one strike against her and she didn't need a strike two.

Usually Madalyn didn't get a chance to take in the scenery, because she had to concentrate on driving the snowmobile. Today Drake was doing the driving, giving Madalyn time to gaze at her surroundings.

The snowy, ice-capped mountains thrusting up all around them were practically beyond words, though "magnificent" and "gigantic" quickly came to mind.

And "remote" . . .

Madalyn nibbled on her lower lip. She'd never really considered just how far out there she lived. The closest village was an hour's ride by snowmobile. What if something happened? What if she needed a doctor? Or what if some psychotic fan found her? There would be no one to help her and Drake, nobody within miles to even hear their screams.

Stop it. Quit being a drama queen!

You could take the girl out of Hollywood, but you couldn't take Hollywood out of the girl. Being dramatic was as much a part of her personality as Drake's conspiracy theories were part of hers.

She shivered as her gaze flicked from one icy mountaintop to the next. Wrapping the polar bear skin more securely around her, she ignored the tiny voice inside that warned her something ominous would happen, and turned her attention back to Drake.

MADALYN LED HER NEW, and thankfully female, goat into the corral, then affectionately patted both animals on their heads. "Victoria, I'd like you to meet the newest addition to our family."

"You're still gonna call him Victoria?" Drake wrinkled her nose. "That's just wrong."

"I've been calling him Victoria for weeks. He answers to it. I can't just give him another name."

"Then what'll you call the female?"

"Hmmm . . ."

"Maybe you should give her a male name. Fair is fair. Besides, people might get the wrong idea if they both have female names."

Madalyn rolled her eyes. "Have you ever heard of lesbian goats?"

"Yeah. I think most of them have had partial mastectomies."

"Very funny."

"So anyway, what are you going to name the female?"

Madalyn pondered the question as she inspected the new goat from head to tail. "She kind of looks like a Thor to me."

"Thor?"

"The name of the hero in my first film."

"Ahhh. We're back to *Song of the Viking*." Drake sighed. "Thor, the girl, and Victoria, the boy. I suppose it works in an *Alice in Wonderland* sort of way."

While feeding the goats, Madalyn recalled the day's events. The trip into Zhitana had been fun. She always had a good time with Drake, but being able to hang out sans reporters breathing down their necks had been beyond great. It made her wish her sister would stay forever.

"Alaska is gorgeous."

"Yeah, I know." Madalyn glanced up and smiled. "Every time I leave the cabin, I have a hard time remembering I'm still in the United States. It's a different world in the Arctic."

"That it is. I hate to leave it."

Something wrenched in the vicinity of her heart. Realistically, Madalyn knew her younger sister wouldn't stay in Alaska forever, but she wasn't quite ready to give her up yet, either. CACW could wait. This time was for the Simon sisters.

"Why don't we drive down to the coast and see if we can spot any whales?" Drake asked.

Madalyn appreciated the change in topic. Thinking about her sister going back to Utah was depressing. "That could be fun. I've never seen a whale, except on TV."

Drake nodded. "Same here."

"Then let's do it! I'll go get the keys to the snowmobile."

"Don't forget your polar bear fur. It'll keep you warm."

Madalyn sighed at the reminder of the ugly thing. She tossed a golden-red curl over her shoulder. "Fine. But if we run into any of its living relatives and they want to know why I'm wearing their cousin, I'm pointing in your direction."

OTAR AND HIS MEN had walked for miles and seen nothing. No foot impressions, no markings left behind by Outsider vehicle tires—no nothing. He scanned the terrain once more, his dark eyes alert. If the warriors of Army had come this far north, they had left it without a trace.

"Iiro!" Otar barked.

"Aye, milord?"

Before Toki had risen to the throne, he had been called that title by all and sundry. Now only a few addressed him thusly, those who thumbed their noses at Toki in secret.

"You've seen nothing?" Otar inquired, knowing the answer but wanting a verbal confirmation.

"Nay."

After receiving the same answer from Luukas, Otar said, "there's no point in continuing this search. There hasn't been any new snowfall in days. Had the Outsider Army come through here, we would have seen some proof by now."

The trio of men started back toward their world, careful to cover up their foot impressions as they walked. Another two hours and they'd be safely ensconced inside Lokitown, the capital of New Sweden. Until then, they would remain alert, prepared for any eventuality.

Otar's gaze continued to scan the horizon. He wouldn't relax until he and his men had made it back to Lokitown without espying an Outsider. Were they to spot one en route, the enemy would be killed. No Outsiders came this far north—ever. If one came now it could only mean trouble.

"I've heard whisperings," Luukas said in a low voice, "that the Revolution will begin in two fortnights. Is it true, milord?"

"You know I cannot discuss this," Otar rumbled. "Just be prepared to battle at a moment's notice."

"The *valar* are surfacing," Iiro pointed out.

Otar glanced toward the icy waters, a slight smile forming on his lips. *Valar*—whales—he'd always loved them. So
gigantic, yet so graceful. Much like a Viking.

His thoughts turned back to war, his gaze still on the
water giants. The whisperings Luukas had heard were true,
and he wondered who would be foolish enough to discuss
strategy with anyone outside Lord Ericsson's inner circle.
Though Otar trusted Luukas, none from the inner circle
should be loose-lipped with anyone—not even with under-
lings they placed their faith in.

Two fortnights and the Revolution would begin. Any
warrior or soldier in his right mind would be dreading it. Yet
Otar felt no trepidation.

Excitement. Eagerness. The desire for vengeance. But no
fear.

His jaw tightened. He hoped *he* delivered the death blow
to Toki; the bastard had put his family through so much. For
himself, Otar did not care. But for his mother and twin sister, he cared mightily.

Annikki, Otar's mother, had begged him not to take
part in the Revolution. She cared naught for vengeance and
didn't want to lose her only son. As much as he grieved for
her possible loss, Otar knew the Revolution was his destiny.

Mayhap death was his destiny, too.

It had been that knowledge that had kept him from
seeking a bride on the marriage auction block for all these
years. At thirty-four, he was well past the age when he
should have taken a wife.

Some rebels, like Luukas, married and reproduced so their lineage could continue after their deaths. To each their own, Otar supposed—but he still felt it was wrong to force a wife to your side, get her with child, then leave her without a mate to help raise the babe.

"Milord," Iiro whispered, breaking Otar from his thoughts. He came to a sudden stop and jumped behind a nearby boulder. Immediately on guard, Otar and Luukas followed suit.

"An Outsider?" Otar murmured, his muscles tensing from behind the rock, preparing for battle.

"Two."

Damn it. "Tell me their position."

Iiro gave him his answer. Otar retrieved two blades from his braes, ready to hurl them with deadly accuracy. Primed for battle, he crouched down and motioned for his men to follow him.

Chapter Five

"*They are breathtaking,*" Drake sighed. "Pristine mammoths living in an environment that is untainted by Big Brother and his chemicals."

Madalyn wouldn't have put it in those words precisely, but she got the point and more than agreed. She'd never seen anything so big and beautiful in her life. TV didn't do the whales a lick of justice.

"They've got a great life," Madalyn mused. She pushed the polar bear skin off her head, letting her golden-red curls spring free. "They swim, sleep, have sex, and eat. Where do I sign up?"

"They aren't hunted by the news media vultures, but

there are plenty of poachers out there hunting and killing them on a daily basis." Drake snapped dozens of photos with her digital camera. "I hope this damn camera's memory card doesn't run out of space," she muttered.

"That's sad," Madalyn said quietly, feeling a sense of camaraderie with the whales. She knew all too well what it felt like to have a bounty on your head. "People disgust me."

"That's another CACW motto."

"Huh."

"We better get back to the cabin," Drake said suddenly, making Madalyn look over at her quizzically.

"Why?"

"I don't know. Just a weird feeling in my belly."

They started walking toward the showmobile.

"Is this like the time we were visiting Mom and Dad and you wouldn't drive down US-31 because you were convinced the cows in Old Willy's pasture were possessed by the devil?"

"It wasn't the devil himself," Drake sniffed defensively. "It was just some kind of evil spirit."

"Right."

"It was my twenty-first birthday and I'd had too much to drink."

"And smoke."

Drake frowned. "I get the point! And *noooo,* it's not like that."

"Or how about that dream you had about Aunt Benny? You made us drag an old lady for a three-mile hike across town because you were certain that her car was going to explode."

"Well, we didn't get in the car, did we? Who's to say what would have happened if we had?"

"Hmmm . . ."

"Look," Drake said, annoyed, "I follow my gut instincts. Sometimes they're right and sometimes they're wrong, but I always follow them." Her boots crunched over the snow. "It's kept me alive, and you unfound, thus far."

Madalyn conceded the point. "I'm just teasing you." She smiled and tucked one of her little sister's silky black tresses behind her ear. "I love you just the way you are. Paranoid schizophrenic or not."

Drake half snorted and half laughed. "Gee, thanks. I think." She stilled, her expression growing serious. "We need to get to the snowmobile *now.*"

Something in the way she'd said "now" made Madalyn nervous. The word had come out almost as a plea—something Drake never made. "Okay," she breathed out. Her gaze darted around as the hair at the nape of her neck began to rise. "Let's go."

"I don't think you will be going anywhere, wench," a low, masculine voice growled in a thick accent.

Madalyn gasped as a powerful, callused hand grabbed her neck from behind and wrapped around her throat. Her eyes widened and her heart raced, threatening to beat out of her chest. She opened her mouth to scream, but his other palm slapped mercilessly over her mouth.

"Who are you? A warrior from Army?" he gritted out

from behind her. Hot breath blew against her neck. *"How did you find us?"*

She had no idea what he was talking about and was too scared to care. His hand prevented her from answering, anyway. He must have remembered that, for he removed it a second later.

Her terrified gaze shot over to Drake. Her sister was being manhandled by two huge men, both of them trying to wrestle her to the ground. "Get off me!" Drake bellowed. "Let me go!"

"I asked who you are," the menacing voice demanded. He tightened his hold around her neck, causing her throat to gurgle and her forehead to perspire. "'Tis wise do you answer me."

The fact that he spoke in antiquated, heavily accented English barely registered. Madalyn was too hysterical to give his speech much thought.

She was going to die!

"M-my name is M-Madalyn," she wheezed, gasping for air. "Please—you're hurting me."

One minute he was standing behind her, threatening to strangle the life out of her, and the next she was being jerked around to face him, the polar bear skin she wore falling to the ground. She couldn't help but struggle for breath when she got her first look at him.

Frightening was too mild a word.

Towering over her by almost a foot, he was as heavily muscled as he was tall. Though his body was mostly covered by animal furs, she could feel the power in his grasp. His hair was black and hung just past his shoulders. A braid snaked from either temple to the back of his head, keeping his hair from falling into his eyes. And those eyes . . .

Black, ruthless slits. No mercy to be found there.

Their gazes clashed. The man stilled, his muscles cording. His eyes widened almost imperceptibly, recognition dawning. "Victoria?" he said, puzzled.

The name of the heroine in *Song of the Viking*. He knew who she was.

Madalyn's hysteria rose. "If you do anything to harm me or my sister, the government will kill you!" she spat. She didn't know if that was true, but desperate times called for desperate words. "If you know who I am, then you know I speak the truth!"

His nostrils flared and he stared at her surreally, as if he couldn't believe she was standing there. Then his gaze narrowed, his eyelids growing heavy with telltale arousal.

Oh no, Madalyn thought, terror engulfing her. *What do I do?*

His eyes widened and his entire body started shaking. Gurgling sounds issued from his throat.

Madalyn instinctively took a step back out of his clutches, wondering if he was having a seizure. Could fate and timing be that wonderful for a change?

He fell to the ground a moment later, incapacitated. Drake—good ol' survivalist Drake!—stood behind him. Wielding a stun gun, she stood amid the three felled bodies like a female Dirty Harry.

Yes! Yes! Yes!

"Let's get out of here," Drake said shakily, sounding more terrified child than accomplished heroine. "I don't know how long the jolts will last."

Those words snapped Madalyn out of her trancelike state. Taking her sister's hand, they ran to the snowmobile as fast as their feet would carry them.

"Kom hit, lilla flicka," growled the biggest man, the one who had recognized Madalyn as Victoria.

His dark head came up, those black eyes narrowing as he began crawling toward her. She freaked out.

"Hurry!" Madalyn screamed, her entire body shaking. "Put the key in the damn ignition!"

"I'm trying!" Drake yelled back, her voice frantic. Shaky hands fumbled with the keys. "Shit!"

The snowmobile roared to life. The felled man on the ground roared in fury.

Her entire body trembling, Madalyn sighed with relief as the snowmobile raced off, leaving their attackers far behind. Green eyes round, she worried her bottom lip, watching the strange man with the strange accent until he was well out of sight.

OTAR HAD NEVER FELT LIKE MORE OF A FOOL. He'd been so taken aback by the discovery that he'd managed to capture his Victoria that he had behaved more the love-struck boy than the seasoned warrior.

And now look at me, he thought, disgusted. He pulled

himself up off the ground, a growl of rage erupting from his throat. His only solace was in knowing that Victoria's sister had managed to take out all three of them. 'Twould keep Iiro and Luukas from carrying humiliating tales back to the Underground.

"We must seize them," Iiro ground out, pulling himself to his feet. "Before they tell others of us."

Otar nodded. He could only pray to Odin they were not too late.

"Kom, så sticker vi." *Let's go.* His gaze honed in on the telltale tracks left behind by the vehicle the wenches had escaped in. "Before there is snowfall and their trail is lost to us."

Iiro and Luukas followed closely behind. Otar's jaw tightened, adrenaline pumping through every muscle. He had never looked forward to hunting anyone with the eagerness he now possessed.

Victoria—Madalyn . . .

His cock stiffened in his braes. She would belong to *him.*

Chapter Six

"Mayday! Mayday! Hello? We've got a one-niner-niner! This is an emergency, you idiots!"

Madalyn chewed at the tip of one acrylic nail as she watched her sister wear a circle on the kitchen floor. Nobody at CACW knew they were in trouble yet. The longer it took to reach them, the more nervous she became.

This wasn't good, she realized, walking toward the window and peering out of it again. Those men might already be looking for them! If Drake couldn't get someone from CACW on the line pronto, they would have to abandon the cabin and head toward Zhitana.

"Well?" Madalyn whispered. "Anything?"

"No. I still don't have a signal. I don't know what to do!"

"We have to leave, Drake. You can keep trying them while we drive toward an Inuit village."

Drake nodded. "Yes," she mumbled, her gaze darting around as if searching for something. "You're right."

"What are you looking for?"

"The camera."

Madalyn pointed toward a chair. "I threw it there when we first arrived. Why do you want it now?"

"Those men stopped us for a reason."

"Yeah, it's called murder! Or rape and murder." Madalyn shivered. "Let's just get out of here, Drake. The longer we stay put, the more freaked out I get."

"Hang on a second," she said, fumbling with the digital camera. "I think there was more to that little attack than meets the eye. Did you notice the odd clothing they wore under their polar bear skins?"

"No, I never saw anything but the furs. I did notice how funny they talked, though."

"Funny?"

"Yeah." Madalyn frowned thoughtfully. "They had thick accents, and their English was . . . odd."

"I know what you mean. I just can't pinpoint why it was odd."

Madalyn was silent for a moment. "It was very Old World. Like they still lived in the 1500s or something."

"Yeah," Drake breathed out. She swallowed hard. "How weird is that?"

"Very weird. But we can discuss this on the way to Zhitana. I want to leave!"

"Hang on a second, I think I found something. I did! Come look!"

Madalyn raced over to the other side of the room. Peering over her sister's shoulder, she saw something in one of the digital photographs. Namely, the three gigantic, odd-speaking men. Their images weren't readily apparent unless you knew what you were looking for, but they were definitely there.

"They didn't want to be photographed," Madalyn murmured, her eyes widening. "I wonder what they were doing that they didn't want to be spotted?"

"I don't know and hopefully we will never find out."

"Right. And on that note, let's get the hell out of here."

"I want to hide the camera first," Drake insisted, glancing around. "I wonder where we can put it so nobody can find it."

Madalyn just wanted to leave. "Who cares about the damn camera? Let's *go* before they find us!"

"I can't get a hold of CACW," Drake pointed out, "but eventually they will wonder why I haven't radioed in and they *will* come searching for us. I need to leave something behind. Just in case . . ." She sighed. "You know what I'm saying."

Madalyn briefly closed her eyes against her sister's words. It didn't bode well if Drake believed it was possible for the three men to catch them again. "The third floorboard comes up. There's a small hiding place below it, large enough to hold the camera."

Drake found Madalyn's hiding place immediately. Securing the camera between a set of diamond earrings and a matching diamond tennis bracelet, she closed the floorboard and looked to Madalyn.

"Okay. Grab the keys and let's get out of here."

IT FELT LIKE IT WAS TAKING FOREVER to reach Zhitana. Worse yet, the fuel level of the snowmobile was getting dangerously low. Another fifteen minutes and they would be out of gas. Madalyn could only pray that the remote Eskimo village appeared over the horizon very soon.

Darkness comes early to the tundra in the winter months, and December was no exception. Madalyn's teeth chattered and there were goosebumps on her arms despite the animal furs she was enveloped in. She cast her gaze warily about, the once beautiful snow-covered mountains taking on a very sinister, ugly appearance in her mind.

She should have paid attention when her gut instincts had told her something bad would happen out here on the isolated, rugged terrain. Drake always valued her gut instincts and Madalyn should have valued her own rather than chalking up her eerie foreboding to being a drama queen.

There's no point in going through the "if only's." What's done is done.

The only thing of importance now was getting to help. The only thing that mattered was surviving.

Madalyn hadn't prayed since she was a little girl. She decided that wasn't a good thing. She also decided to remedy the situation at once.

Please, God, let us make it to Zhitana. Please let Drake and me be okay. Or at least Drake. If you have to take one of us, let it be me.

Drake would strangle her if she knew that Madalyn was asking for her sister's life to be spared at the expense of her own. Of course, Madalyn would have strangled Drake if she knew her sister had been praying for the same thing, but in reverse.

AGAINST ALL ODDS, they made it to Zhitana. Madalyn had never been so glad to see bartered goat milk and cheese in her life. It tasted better than nachos and piña coladas. Well, maybe not, but it was close, she decided.

All this time later and Drake had still not managed to get a signal out. The longer they went without reaching CACW, the more they both feared there was something unfixable about the mobile phone.

"You can stay in this hut," an elderly Eskimo woman told Madalyn and Drake. "Nobody will know you are here except the villagers. I will send one of the boys into a nearby town to get you help."

"Thank you," Madalyn gushed in relief. "We can't thank you enough!"

The old woman waved the praise away. "Don't thank me yet," she muttered, showing them into the hut. She wore an intricately knitted sweater over an animal skin dress. Her silver hair, coarse with age, fell down to her waist. Brown leather boots completed the ensemble. "Get some sleep. I'll be back in the morning."

Madalyn waited for the tent door to slap shut behind the old woman before she turned to Drake. "What do you think she meant by that?" she whispered, worried.

"Meant by what?" Drake asked over a mouthful of cheese and bread.

"She said, 'Don't thank me yet.' What did she mean by that?"

Drake sighed. "And you call me paranoid? I'm sure she just meant not to thank her until help comes and we're officially out of harm's way."

Madalyn hoped Drake was right.

Walking to the door flap, she opened it a tiny crack to take a quick peek through. The sight that greeted her on the other side made her pulse skyrocket. She sucked in a breath.

There, just a few feet away, stood their three attackers. Worse yet, they were conversing with the old Inuit woman as though they were longtime friends. She saw the men hand the crone what looked to be a bag of coins, then the old woman turned and pointed toward their hut.

Oh. My. God.

"Drake!" she whispered, growing hysterical. "Come here. Now!"

Drake was there in a heartbeat, peering over Madalyn's shoulder. She gasped. "Oh no. Oh damn!"

"What do we do?"

"I don't know! Let's find a way out of here!"

They had to be quick. The three men were already heading toward the tent at a brisk pace.

"Let's crawl under the back of the tent and run!" Madalyn told Drake. "It's our only chance!"

Scurrying toward the back of the hut, Drake picked up the hem of the tent's skirt and held it up for Madalyn. Once through, Madalyn did the same for Drake. After both women were out, they took off running in the dark.

Chapter Seven

Go faster, Madalyn! Faster, damn you!

Madalyn sprinted as quickly as she possibly could. The problem was, there wasn't anywhere to go. It was dark, frigid, and there was no shelter to be had. No forests thick with trees to hide in, no boulders to dash behind.

The sound of footsteps and male shouts caused the hair at the nape of her neck to stand up. They had been spotted!

"Fånga dom!"

"Låt dom inte komma undan!"

"Keep running!" Drake yelled.

Madalyn refused to give in to the hopelessness that threatened to swamp her. If these men meant to kill her and

Drake, they would at least make sure the bastards had their work cut out for them.

Her breathing grew labored, and perspiration broke out on her forehead and between her breasts. Ice-cold terror set in anew. She couldn't believe this was happening. From Hollywood darling to dead woman in the blink of an eye.

It's not over until it's over . . .

She could hear the crunch of heavy boots on snow growing closer; she could all but feel the hot breath of her pursuer on her neck.

He had recognized her back at the ocean. Worse yet, he had wanted her. Madalyn had seen that look in the eyes of too many male groupies to mistake it for anything other than lust.

"Kom hit, lilla flicka," he called, far too close for her liking.

"Run faster!" Drake screeched. "The big one is closing in on you!"

Madalyn braved a look over her shoulder. Her eyes widened and she whimpered. He was only about four giant steps from reaching her.

"Noooo!" she cried out as his rough hands seized her hips from behind. She screamed as she fell to the ground, his heavy body coming down hard on top of hers.

Madalyn tried to yell for help, but the wind had been knocked out of her. She gasped for air.

"Let me go!" Drake bellowed, trying to get away from

the other two men. This time she didn't succeed. This time they managed to wrestle her to the ground.

"You are fine," a deep, heavily accented voice murmured to Madalyn. "Be still." She could feel his erection pressed against her buttocks.

Oh God.

Madalyn didn't know whether to scream, cry, or both. She didn't want to die. She didn't want to be raped. Sweet God, she'd never been so frightened.

"Shhh," her captor said softly, shifting his weight to his knees. "You will be fine, do you just lie there and right your breathing."

"What do you want from us?" Madalyn rasped out.

Weak, she cocked her head and glanced over her right shoulder as best she could. Black eyes locked with scared green ones. She felt this close to passing out.

"What do you want?" she asked again, her voice catching.

"I want you."

"IF YOU THINK WE'RE GOING DOWN EASY, think twice, bastards."

Otar ignored the vile-tongued sister of Madalyn and kept his prisoners moving. Soon they would reach the hidden door that led to the hidden world below.

Capturing the wenches had been child's play. Otar had tracked the vehicle's tire impressions to a cabin, searched the dwelling, found nothing, then followed the second set of tracks into Zhitana. The rest had been easy. The only objective left was to seize and destroy their picture-taker, which Outsiders referred to as a camera.

The picture-taker had not been in the cabin—they'd torn it apart looking for the bedamned thing. It had to be in the possession of either Madalyn or her sister. With the wenches firmly under his dominion and the camera under theirs—for now—the secret of the Underground would remain.

Not even the wizened Inuit woman knew of the Underground; she thought his men to be fur traders. He had told her he wanted to find the two wenches because they had stolen furs from his home. A lie, mayhap, but a necessary one.

"Wait until you're asleep," Drake taunted. "We'll get you."

Otar turned his attention to Madalyn's sister. Amused by her bluster, he hid a smile.

"Oh, yes, we will get you!"

She made a gesture that resembled a she-devil taking a pair of scissors to their man-parts. Iiro frowned, not having a care for the mental picture she conjured up in him. The "snip-snip" sound she made, followed by a demonic chuckle, apparently set fire to his temper.

"Do you ever shut up, wench?" Iiro bellowed. "You're easy on the eyes, but hard on the ears."

She blushed. A surprisingly modest affectation for one so loud.

"I will not shut up for you," she hissed. Her green eyes narrowed into slits. "Just wait until they find out we've been stolen. Oh, yes, they *will* find out! My sister is famous, you know. When word spreads of her disappearance, the people of this nation will not rest until she is found!"

"Enough," Madalyn said softly to her sister. "Don't waste your breath on these . . . these . . . these . . . really bad people!"

Otar snorted. "'Tis the best you can do?" he drawled. He was teasing her, but she didn't yet know him well enough to discern as much. "I daresay your sister is much better at baiting."

That got her goat. A long, impressive string of bawdy words gushed from her rouge lips like a waterfall. He was amused, but he didn't smile.

Madalyn came to a halt. "What do you want with us?" she spat. "If you plan to kill us, could you at least have the decency to just do it already and end the glorious anticipation?"

"Amen!" the she-devil chimed in.

"Cease your prattling," Iiro scolded Drake.

"Why do you talk so funny?" Drake gritted out. "In case you don't keep up with the news, bucko, the year is 2006, not 1506."

"Aye? So?"

"So people don't use words like 'aye' anymore! That vocabulary went the way of pirates. Extinct. Sunken ship, mates."

"To answer your question," Otar said to Madalyn, ignoring Drake, "you will not be killed." He took her by the arm and prodded her back into moving.

"Then what do you want with us?"

He shrugged, a seemingly unconcerned gesture. "Our people need more females."

Both wenches were dead quiet as they locked gazes with each other and absorbed the implication this news had to their future lives. It was Madalyn who broke the silence first.

Her hand flew to cover her heart. "Sweet Jesus, just kill me now!"

"Me, too!" her sister piped in. "I'd rather lie in bed with Big Brother than fuck one of you psychos!"

"Oh my God," Madalyn squealed, hysteria visibly engulfing her. She looked dazed. Her body appeared to tremble. Otar wondered if he would have been wise to keep his thoughts to himself until they reached Lokitown. "Please tell me this isn't happening!"

"You would rather fuck your brother?" Iiro asked Drake, astonished.

Madalyn's face went red with fury and mayhap a bit of frustration. "She—*we*—don't have a brother, idiot!"

"Do not speak to Iiro thusly, wench," Otar calmly chided her. "Leastways, she did say she would rather—"

"I know what she said," Madalyn snapped. "Just never mind." She waved him away, dismissing him, then rubbed her temples as if her head had gone to aching. "I'm too tired to deal with you."

Iiro and Luukas looked at Otar with round eyes. Neither man had ever heard anyone, male or female, speak to him in such an insulting manner. 'Twas a foolhardy thing to do.

He found himself amused that wee Madalyn spoke to him in the way she wanted to. Of course, she didn't yet know who he was to the rebels of New Sweden. But that didn't mean he could let the slight go uncorrected.

Otar came to a sudden stop and whirled Madalyn around to face him. Her eyes widened as she braved a look up at his face. "Do not ever speak to me like that again in front of my men. Say what you will in privacy, but watch your tongue in front of others."

She glanced away. He tightened his hold on her arms until she looked back up at him.

"Okay," she said, a hint of fear mixing with the anger in her voice. "I'm . . . sorry."

Arrogantly appeased, he forced her to walk again. "As you should be."

Chapter Eight

It had been a long day. Madalyn couldn't recall ever being so exhausted. She and Drake had been captured, escaped, then proceeded to flee to Zhitana, only to be recaptured. That had been enough. Walking for miles made her weariness all the more grueling.

That wasn't the worst of it. Finding out that these men intended to keep them as some sort of sex slaves was enough to take her mind off her fatigue and keep it honed in on their less than desirable fates.

She couldn't believe it. A part of Madalyn still believed this was all a bad dream from which she would soon awaken.

Even Drake was shell-shocked. When they'd first been

captured, her little sister had started out on the fiery, brave side, but the farther the group traveled, the warier she looked. She hadn't said a word in well over an hour, which worried Madalyn. It wasn't like Drake.

Don't worry, honey. If I can find a way out of this mess, I'll get us back to civilization.

Madalyn stole a glance at her captor, whom the other two men called Otar.

What kind of a name was that? What language did they converse in when they didn't want Drake and her to understand what they were saying? Madalyn had traveled the world over, but she'd never heard *anyone* speak quite like their captors did.

His face had a chiseled, hawkish appearance. Everything about him looked hard. His body, his demeanor, his stoic expression—merciless.

A chill worked down her spine. She knew he would never willingly let her go. "Defeat" was no more in his vocabulary than "aye" was in hers.

Ironically, Otar was a ruggedly handsome man, quite striking in a rough-and-tumble sort of way. Looks-wise, he was the type of guy she'd dreamt of meeting all those lonely years back in Hollywood: tall, dark, muscular, and handsome. Why would a man like him need to steal a woman? Surely there were females aplenty who wanted him.

He might have *looked* like the mega-macho version of Prince Charming, but he certainly didn't act like him. Unless her mother had read her the wrong fairy tale, Madalyn was pretty certain that kidnapping, coercion—and possibly rape—had never entered into the story.

She sighed, telling herself she was stupid. She should be mentally planning her and Drake's escape, not thinking about things that couldn't be changed.

Still, she couldn't help but wonder why these men had stolen them. Madalyn had assumed they would either let them go or kill them after they retrieved the camera, but nobody had so much as mentioned the digital. She certainly wouldn't offer any information. The hidden camera was, at present, their best hope at being found. Their *only* hope.

"We are almost there," she heard Iiro tell Drake. He propped her up, helping her walk. "You can rest anon."

Madalyn wondered where they were being taken. She could only pray it was a place where they'd find someone—anyone—who was willing to help them escape.

"Dörren är där borta," Iiro remarked to Otar.

"Ja," Otar replied. He cleared his throat, then switched to English, or his version of it, anyway. "'Tis done. We are here," he announced.

Madalyn frowned. She glanced around but saw nothing. Looking to Drake, she watched for her sister's reaction. Drake appeared to be every bit as confused as she was.

"I don't get it," Madalyn said. "There's nothing here but snow . . ." She glanced up. "And really big mountains."

"You live up there?" Drake asked, disgust in her voice. "No cabins or even huts? We're accustomed to the finer things in life, boys. This will never work."

Madalyn found herself snorting a semilaugh for the first time since they were captured. It was great to hear Drake running her mouth again. And it was amusing, despite the situation, that she would ever claim to be used to "the finer things in life." Madalyn, yes, but not Drake. Her sister would choose a harsh, rural existence in an underground extremist science facility over a life of luxury, or even comfort, any day of the week.

Glancing over at Otar, Madalyn was unnerved to find him staring at her again. There was a peculiar gleam in his eyes. It wasn't lust, love, hate, or any other identifiable emotion.

"You are used to the finer things in life, Madalyn?" Otar asked.

The answer seemed important to him. How very odd. "I am," she said simply.

He continued to stare at her. She didn't know what he was really asking, but she didn't care for suspense. "Why do you ask?"

He blinked, then looked away. "I was but curious."

"So," Drake interrupted, "you live up on top of this mountain?"

"Nay," Otar replied, finding Madalyn's gaze once more. "We live under them."

Madalyn stilled. Her eyes widened. *Under them?*

She shivered, then quickly looked to Drake. Her sister's face had gone rather pale for a woman so tan. She knew better than anybody that being taken down into such a remote, secret location didn't bode well for their escape.

This wasn't happening. It just couldn't be happening.

Her heart beating like mad, Madalyn turned to dash away. Otar's unyielding hands stopped her in her tracks before she could take one step.

"Help us!" Madalyn wailed. "Somebody hel—"

A callused palm flew to her mouth, covering it. "Shhh," Otar told her, trying to calm her down. "All will be well."

Madalyn raged against her subjugator with every bit of strength she could muster. She kicked him with her shins, buried her nails into his arms until she drew blood, and tried repeatedly to jerk away from him. It didn't help. Nothing helped.

The next thing she knew, she was being hoisted up over Otar's shoulder and carried toward the mountain.

"No!" she heard Drake scream. *"Noooooo!"*

The men carried the women through a hidden door, then the impenetrable boulder portal was forced shut behind them, chained and locked. As they were carried down the inside of a carved-out mountain, where their pleas for help would never be heard, Drake screamed like a banshee. Madalyn did the same, but from behind her captor's powerful hand.

"KEEP YOUR EYES OPEN and your mouth shut," Madalyn murmured to Drake. "Don't get in any arguments. We need to pay close attention to everything around us so we know what we're dealing with."

"I never thought it would be *you* giving *me* survivalist

advice," Drake whispered back. She squeezed her hand. "But thanks, Maddie Mae. I'm big-time freaking out."

So was Madalyn, but she kept that to herself. She was just grateful Otar had finally put her down and let her walk with her sister. Not that it was doing either of them a lick of good. It was pitch-black, and the only light sources were being emitted by the torches their captors were carrying. As far as she could tell, there wasn't anything significant to see, anyway.

"Watch your footing, wenches," Iiro commanded them. "'Tis tricky through here, lots of curves."

Wenches. They'd been called that so many times in the past several hours that it was starting to sound normal. Where on earth had they learned their English?

So many questions and no answers. Madalyn needed to quickly put the puzzle pieces together so she and Drake could find a way home . . . wherever that was.

She had tried to find her place in Hollywood but had ended up feeling like an emotional shell. She had thought she was experiencing the real thing in Alaska, only to become a hostage. Madalyn dejectedly realized that she hadn't had a real home since her mom and dad died. That was so long ago, she couldn't remember what it felt like.

Her back straightened. She told herself to stop the self-pity. Anyplace where she was free was superior to being here, where she was a captive. As long as Otar controlled her, she would never find that elusive, magical thing called home. Hollywood might not have fit the bill, but at least she could still dream about it there.

"Ouch!"

Madalyn gasped as she tripped over a small rock. Luckily, she caught her footing before she fell face-first on the ground. Coming to a shaky halt, she stopped to rub her ankle. Otar, who had been in the rear lest they try to escape, quickly caught up to her.

"Are you injured?" he asked softly.

Something in his voice said he genuinely cared about the answer, which threw Madalyn for a loop. The expression in his eyes, partially illuminated by the flame of the torch he wielded, underscored the sincerity of his worry.

"No," she reassured him. "I think I just bruised my ankle."

"I will carry you."

"I'm fine. Really."

He didn't look convinced, but thankfully, he let it slide. "Take my hand. I will guide you the rest of the way, or least-ways until we reach light."

Madalyn chewed on her bottom lip. She didn't want the familiarity of hand-holding with him, but he would carry her if she refused him. Being toted around like a sack of potatoes was less familiar, but it was also more embarrassing, not to mention dehumanizing.

"You okay, sis?" she heard Drake whisper from some-where in front of her.

"She is fine," Otar answered for her. "I will care for her."

Madalyn tensed up. She prayed that, for once, her little sister would keep her mouth shut. She subtly blew out a breath when she realized Drake was indeed biting her tongue.

"Take my hand," Otar murmured.

She swallowed roughly as she looked down at his hand, which was at least twice the size of hers. His fingers were long and powerful. They looked like they could choke the life out of anyone, and her in particular.

You're back to being a drama queen. You have every right to hate this man, but he hasn't made one move to harm you. At least not yet . . .

Madalyn slid her hand into Otar's grasp. He appeared to be placated, which was probably a good thing.

They walked that way together for another half hour or longer. Truthfully, she found herself glad for accepting his help. The terrain was getting rougher and began sloping steeply downhill.

A chorus of competing sounds reached Madalyn's ears and she frowned trying to pick them apart. Cheers, whistles, voices. *Lots* of voices. Grinding metal. Animals. It sounded like . . .

Civilization?

Her teeth nervously sank into her lower lip. She recalled a reference Otar had made before that inferred there were more of his kind. What had he said again? Her pulse raced as she suddenly remembered.

Our people need more females.

Our people. As in, there were many, many more men like him in the place they were being steered toward. *Oh, damn.*

Light penetrated the darkness, signaling that the end of

the journey was almost here. The sounds and smells grew closer, more pronounced.

Madalyn's legs began to tremble, and she reminded herself of the need to stay calm. She couldn't think rationally when she was worked up.

They rounded a final bend. The path suddenly ended and they were thrust out of the darkness . . .

And into a surreal place she'd never dreamt existed.

"What the . . . ?" Drake muttered. "Holy shit."

"Oh my God," Madalyn whispered. Her heart began to race, her teeth to chatter. Her mouth worked up and down, but it took a long moment to get anything out. "What in the world *is* this place?"

Chapter Nine

" 'Tis called Lokitown," Otar answered. "My home."

Madalyn heard him speaking, but nothing computed. She was too busy staring, unable to believe what she was seeing. This place couldn't be real . . . it just couldn't be.

A few years ago, Madalyn had visited the underground barricade Drake called home. She had thought that tiny place in Utah was an elaborate little getup. The science facility wasn't even in the same ballpark as this fortress. If Drake's open-jawed expression was anything to go by, she was making the same comparison.

The inside of the mountain had been carved out for as high up as the eye could see. In the place of its guts a huge civilization had been erected, a culture that was as advanced in appearance as it was archaic.

The people dressed like actors in a movie that had been set in medieval times. Animals roamed about, stopping to eat hay and oats that were scattered around on the floor, further bringing to mind life in antiquity.

In striking contrast to the Old World atmosphere, there were also modern, if crude, conveniences. Elevators, computer-generated voices speaking in that odd tongue, and a highly advanced machine that grew fruit and vegetables as though it were a living womb.

Unbelievable.

Madalyn blinked. It took her a minute to grasp the full picture, to understand what it was she was staring at. In essence, she was watching people shop at their version of a mall.

Men and women walked hand in hand, laughing and happy. The males were dressed like ancient Vikings, the females like sex kittens. They flitted from primitive store to primitive store, their demeanors festive. Fruits and vegetables here, odd jewelry and clothing there.

"What is going on?" Drake rasped out. "How could a place like this exist without somebody knowing about it?"

"There are more such bartering colonies on different levels of New Sweden," Otar announced. "This is one of the favored of my people."

"New Sweden?" Madalyn dragged her dumbfounded gaze away and up to her captor. "You are all Swedish, then?"

"Vikings."

She swallowed. "The Vikings have been dead for eons."

"Apparently not."

"Great," Drake snarled. "Nothing like being captured by retro rapists and pillagers to pep up a slow day."

Madalyn didn't know what to say to that. She also didn't know how much longer she could stand up. Her belly was buzzing with butterflies and her legs felt as rubbery as wet noodles.

Thankfully, Otar said, taking her by the elbow, "You may ask questions of your new home later. Right now you need to rest."

"DID YOU HEAR what that bastard said to you?" Drake asked. She sounded as hysterical as Madalyn felt. "He said, and I quote, 'You may ask questions of your new home later.' *Your new home.* Hells bells, Maddie Mae! What do we do?"

She wished she knew. Right now she was so dazed she could barely recall her own name.

Madalyn frowned as she tucked a golden-red curl behind an ear. "We've got to think, Drake, and we've got to do it fast. There's no telling how long they'll let us stay together."

Drake's eyes were unblinking. "For all we know they might separate us for good, never to lay eyes on each other again."

Fear lanced through Madalyn. She hadn't thought of that possibility, but it was a real one. Especially considering the fact they wanted the camera. It was the first thing Otar had asked for when they'd arrived at this room.

Their captors believed that either Madalyn or Drake had the digital camera hidden in their clothes, but were refusing to hand it over. Otar had become irate when Madalyn swore to him that the camera was not with them. She had told him part of the truth—that it was back at her cabin—but hadn't revealed its precise location.

"What if they separate us until we tell them where to find the digital?" Madalyn asked. "I think we should tell them rather than be separated."

"No way!"

Madalyn huffed. "You said yourself that nobody would even realize their images were in that photograph unless they knew to look."

"Hopefully CACW will figure it out."

"And if they don't?"

Drake sighed and glanced away. "I don't know."

Madalyn dropped the subject for the time being. Her gaze darted about the tiny room they were locked in.

It was small and sparse, but the bed was comfortable and the food that had been left for them was tasty. At first, Drake had been afraid to eat it. Madalyn had been too hungry to care.

Other than the bed, there wasn't much more in the room. A wooden chest that doubled as a nightstand was pushed up against one side of the bed and a lamp was on the other side.

Otar, Iiro, and Luukas had been gone for over an hour, but Madalyn deeply suspected that at least Otar and Iiro would return soon. She'd have to be a raging moron to not realize that Otar wanted her, and she'd seen Iiro gaze lustfully at Drake more than a few times. Either that or he'd been fantasizing about ways to shut her up.

She began to pace. Their time alone together could be very limited.

"Do you know what I think?" Drake asked, sitting up on the bed.

"What?"

"I think there are only two reasonable explanations for who these psychos are."

Madalyn stopped to listen. "Go on," she breathed out.

Drake narrowed her eyes, which meant she was very serious. "The first possibility is that Big Brother runs this show, and these people brought us here to turn us into those medieval Stepford Wives we saw in that shopping place."

"That doesn't seem very plausible." Just once, could her sister not have a conspiracy theory that involved the government or aliens as an explanation?

"I don't think so, either," Drake agreed. "And that leaves only one conclusion." She waved a hand toward the door. "These weirdos are aliens."

Apparently, she couldn't. "Drake—"

"I know how crazy it sounds, Maddie Mae, but think about it for a second. If you don't see my rationale, then I'll explain it to you."

"I don't doubt that."

Drake began checking off the most salient points on her

hand. She raised her first finger. "The men here are *wayyy* taller than normal. And not just one or two of them, but every single man we've encountered." Another finger. "None of the males ever show emotion. Even when they yell at you, they seem to do it à la Leonard Nimoy's Spock."

"Hmmm."

Finger three. "It's impossible for a race of humans to live in such an elaborate civilization without anybody finding out about it."

"How do we know the American government doesn't know about this place?"

She waved that theory away. "Let us just say that CACW knows all."

Madalyn rolled her eyes. "Good grief, Drake, stop it already! These people aren't Big Brother and they aren't aliens, either. They are a bunch of throwbacks that mean to keep us as some sort of sexual chattel." She threw up her arms. "I wish they were aliens! Right now getting my brains sucked out through a straw by little green men sounds more palatable than what we both know is coming!"

Drake's gaze fell to the floor. She looked more the scared, lost little girl than the together woman she typically was.

"I'm sorry I yelled." Madalyn forced a smile and tried not to cry, though her voice shook a little. "I'm just terribly scared."

"Me, too."

She walked over to the bed and sat down next to her sister. "One way or another, we'll get through this. I promise."

"But how?"

"I don't know, but I do know this . . ."

Drake glanced over to her. "Yeah?"

"Promise me, if you ever get the chance, you will run. Even if it means leaving me behind."

Drake's eyes rounded. "Maddie—"

"It might be our only hope," Madalyn said patiently, but with conviction. "One of us has to break free and get help." She searched her sister's gaze. "Promise me?" she whispered.

Drake stared at her through big eyes. "I promise," she whispered back.

Madalyn nodded. "Hopefully it won't come to that, honey. Maybe we'll get lucky and we can escape together."

"God, I hope so."

"Me, too."

They were quiet for a long while as they sat on the bed together, lost in thought. Madalyn knew the best way to escape was to do the least desirable thing—become familiar with the layout of the entire underground colony.

"Maddie Mae?"

"Yes, Drake?"

"Did you notice how blue Iiro's eyes are?"

"No."

"I did. They're *too* blue." Her eyes narrowed as she lowered her voice to a whisper. "*Alien* blue."

Madalyn sighed. "You're being a paranoid schizophrenic again."

"In the words of a great philosopher, 'Just because you're paranoid, it doesn't mean they aren't out to get you.'"

"Which philosopher?"

"Okay, so I read it on a bumper sticker." She splayed her hands. "Doesn't make it any less true."

HIS JAW TIGHT AND MUSCLES TENSE, Otar vigorously pumped his cock with his hand. Lying on his bed, he fantasized about storming into Madalyn's bedchamber and having his wicked way with her wee body.

'Twas the same fantasy he'd possessed of her for years. The difference now was Madalyn was really here, just a few levels away.

Wanting to give her some time to come to terms with all that had transpired this day, he had taken Madalyn and her sister to Otrygg's dwelling and locked them into a spare bedchamber where they could be alone.

On the morrow, after she'd had time to calm down, Otar would move her into his own dwelling. He feared 'twould never live up to what she was accustomed to, but he had to have her regardless.

Otar had told himself he would only wed after the Revolution, assuming he survived it. Had he not encountered Madalyn, he would have held true to his word. But, Madalyn . . .

If he didn't marry her, then by the laws of New Sweden, another warrior would be permitted to. The thought of any man touching her was enough to make him spit nails.

Putting those thoughts away for the moment, Otar picked up the speed of his masturbation. He moaned as he pretended it was Madalyn's warm, wet pussy milking his shaft.

He came on a loud groan, his hot seed spurting all over his hand and belly. Opening his eyes and steadying his breathing, he reached for a wet rag to clean himself with.

Afterward, he stood up and took a thorough look around his home. He frowned.

Madalyn, accustomed to the finer things in life, would never take a liking to this tiny hole-in-the-wall. Once, many years ago, Otar had lived in a vast dwelling, with every privilege available his for the taking.

But the palatial holding that was rightfully his upon his sire's death had been confiscated the day his cousin came into power. Otar's ancestral home had been gifted to one of Toki's favored lords, a sadistic arse named Nothrum.

Otar's nostrils flared. One day very soon he would reclaim his dwelling.

Mayhap then he would be deserving of Madalyn.

Chapter Ten

"*I am more than a little curious* to find out what transpired aboveground." Nikolas Ericsson's expression was unreadable as he motioned for Otar to follow him. After checking that his men were busy at work in the grindstone, he turned to give Otar his full attention. "The rumormongers, namely Old Myria, are abuzz."

Otar snorted. There was no finer healer in all of New Sweden than Old Myria. There was no finer gossip, either. At ninety and three, she was as feisty as she was wizened.

"I did not find any warriors of Army searching for our stronghold, milord."

"Excellent."

"I did, however, retrieve two Outsider wenches."

"I've heard so. How do you know they are not from Army?"

"I know because I know." An arrogant but true statement. "Ferreting out information and people is what I do, Niko."

And because he was so good at it, Nikolas accepted that answer at face value. If Otar believed they were not from Army, then they were not.

"Then why did you take them?" Nikolas ground out. 'Twas the first time Otar had ever seen his cousin angered with him. "They will both end up on Toki's bedamned auction block! I know *you* will not claim Hunter's Right and wed either of them."

Hunter's Right. 'Twas an old, sacred law that gave unwed warriors the legal claim to a wench they captured, should they desire to marry her. If the warrior was already wed, or didn't covet a union with the captive in question, she was passed on to the auctioneer and placed up for bid to the highest buyer.

Before Toki had come to power, the bride auction block had been a revered Viking tradition. Under their mutual cousin's regime, 'twas a place of humiliation and shame. Forced to stand naked before dozens, sometimes hundreds, of jeering men, the wenches were touched, licked, and fondled as future potential husbands bodily inspected them.

Nikolas refused to take a bride whilst Toki was still in power. Likewise, he forbade his rebel followers from stealing any wenches they did not wish to take to wife, lest they be subjugated to the demeaning bride auction.

"I took the women because their picture-taker possesses images of us on it," Otar replied.

Nikolas stilled. "Did you retrieve it?"

"Nay. We tore apart their dwelling and did not find it. 'Tis on one of their persons and will be retrieved anon."

Lord Ericsson was appeased. "Excellent. I guess you had no choice, then. 'Tis unfortunate they must go to the block, but you did what was right for our people and our way of life."

"Neither wench shall go to the block," Otar told him. "I made a vow to you that I would never subject a female to that. Outsider or not, and I will honor that vow."

"What do you mean? Iiro and Luukas will take them as wives?" Nikolas frowned. "Luukas is already wed."

"Iiro will take one of them to wife."

"And the other?"

"I will take her."

Nikolas looked too stunned to speak, and with reason. Once Otar made up his mind on a subject, he never changed it. But then he'd made the decision not to marry until the Revolution was won before he'd found Madalyn.

His cousin blew out a breath. "I can hardly wait to meet the wench. She must be extraordinary."

"Aye, she is."

Otar kept her identity to himself. If he told Nikolas just who Madalyn was, he would think he'd gone daft. Later, when his new bride was with him, he would introduce them. Once Lord Ericsson got a look at her face, no explanation would be necessary.

Nikolas patted him on the back. "Good work, Otar." He sighed. "I must go. I've my own captive to fret over."

"So I've heard." Otar's eyes held a sly gleam. "The entire colony has heard."

Nikolas grunted.

"I was told your captive will go on the auction block this eve, in about an hour."

"I had no choice but to capture her," Nikolas growled, his voice defensive. "She found the Underground."

Otar searched his expression. "You will not claim Hunter's Right?"

"Nay." His face looked a little disappointed, surprising Otar. 'Twas obvious he'd grown to care for the wench. "I have my reasons."

"I'm certain you do," Otar murmured.

Nikolas frowned. "Concern yourself with your own wench troubles. Be gone."

Otar grinned. "Aye, milord."

FROM INSIDE THE SMALL BEDROOM, Madalyn heard the sound of heavy boots pounding against the dirt-packed floor. Someone was coming. Her heart raced, wondering what would be done with her and Drake.

"Wake up!" she fervently whispered to her sister. "I hear footsteps!"

Drake jarred awake, then jolted upright on the bed. Madalyn quickly took a seat next to her, wanting to appear as nonchalant as possible when the door was opened.

She recalled chapter 10, verse 1 of the CACW manual: *Never show your fear to the enemy.* Easier said than done, but she decided that a two-time Oscar-winning actress should be cut out for the job.

When the door came crashing open and Madalyn saw her huge Viking captor enter the room, she changed her mind. Nobody was cut out for an acting job like this one; his larger-than-life presence was too unnerving. Her pulse picked up.

The first thing she noticed was that Otar had bathed and changed clothes. His face was freshly shaved, the hair at his temples newly braided. He was no longer wearing the polar bear furs, and she got her first good look at his musculature. She nibbled on her bottom lip as she inspected him from head to toe.

He wore a sleeveless shirt fashioned from heavy silver chain-mail, and his tan arms bulged with muscles. Silver bangles encrusted with gems snaked his biceps, delineating the power of his arms. The pants he wore resembled raw, black leather that hadn't been cured to give that glossy appearance. His boots, also black, stopped just above the calves.

Madalyn's gaze flicked up to his face. His expression, always stoic, hadn't changed. There was no way to gauge what he was thinking or feeling, which was probably the most intimidating thing about him. Considering his height, musculature, and the fact that he currently wielded all power over her, that was saying a lot.

She hated to admit it, but he really was handsome. Not cute, passable, or just good-looking, but virilely handsome. Had she met him under different circumstances, she would have wanted him.

Madalyn blinked, angry that she'd even noticed what he looked like.

He was an anomaly, she consoled herself. Bad men should look the part. They weren't supposed to be remotely charismatic and attractive, let alone resemble an avenging god.

"Have you eaten?" Otar asked.

"Yes. It was good," she said uncomfortably. "Thank you."

He nodded. "Then let me come straight to the point."

"I would appreciate that."

"I suppose you would like an explanation of where you are, why you've been brought here, and what will become of you."

"Don't forget about me. I'd like some answers, too," Drake said.

Otar frowned at the interruption. "'Tis no longer my place to instruct you, wench," he said cryptically. "Iiro will be here anon to collect you."

Drake stilled. "*Collect* me?"

"What are you saying?" Madalyn breathed out.

Oh no! They were going to be separated? Was this it,

then? Sick with the knowledge that she might never see her sister again, Madalyn's eyes began to well up with tears. She quickly blinked the tears at bay, refusing to show him how scared she was.

Her back went ramrod-straight. "What's going to happen to Drake?"

"She will be fine, Madalyn," Otar said softly. "You've my word."

She sensed that his word meant a great deal to him. Still, it wasn't very much comfort.

"We don't have the damn camera!" Madalyn blurted out. "I'm not lying!"

"Maddie," Drake bit out warningly.

"Well, we don't! There's no point in separating us if you think you'll retrieve it with the old divide-and-conquer method." She threw her hands up. "We really do not have it."

Otar studied her through hooded eyes. "Come," he finally said to Madalyn, extending his hand. "'Tis time for you to leave with me."

Fear and nerves sent adrenaline rushing through her. Her stomach churned, nausea overwhelming her. Her gaze flashed to Drake, who looked as though she might cry.

"Don't separate us," Madalyn pleaded, ignoring the invitation to take his hand. "Anything but that!"

His expression never wavered, though something in his eyes seemed to soften. "'Tis how it must be, Madalyn." Otar extended his hand once more. "Come with me of your own volition or I will carry you from this bedchamber."

Drake's hand flew up to cover her mouth. She closed her eyes and steadied her breathing.

"Will I see her again?" Madalyn asked Otar.

"Aye. 'Twill be a while, but you will be permitted to see her again."

Drake's eyes flew open. Madalyn's gaze flicked back and forth between her sister and her captor. When she opened her mouth to speak, Drake held up a palm.

"I'll be fine," Drake said. "Go on. I'll see you soon."

Madalyn hesitated, uncertain what to do. She wanted to stay with her sister but realized Otar would remain true to his word. If she didn't leave the room with him willingly, then she'd leave it unwillingly. Either way, she would be forced to go.

She embraced her sister. "Are you sure, sweetheart?" Madalyn whispered.

"Go. Keep him busy," Drake said low so Otar couldn't hear. "I've got plans."

Madalyn's heart skipped a beat. She hugged her little sister one last time, praying that none of her plans got her killed. "I love you, Drake."

"I love you, too. Stay strong."

Madalyn straightened her posture and, taking a deep breath, walked toward the door. Refusing to look at Otar, she glanced back at Drake a final time, her heart in her eyes, and exited the room.

Chapter Eleven

Madalyn quietly followed Otar's lead as he steered her down a long, earthen corridor. She had no idea where he was taking her, but decided against asking. She'd find out soon enough.

She glanced up, taking note of small windows that had been carved into the tall ceilings. The circles were far too tiny to squeeze a body through, but they probably permitted the sun to breach this belowground world during daylight hours.

Otar led Madalyn to an iron elevator. Black and sturdy, it resembled the ones often used at skyscraper construction sites.

"Come," Otar said as they neared it. "I've something to show you."

Madalyn stepped into the elevator. After closing its door, he pushed down a lever and held it in place as the cage soared up several stories. Walking to the back of it, she stared at similar contraptions zinging up and down all over the colony. The underground civilization possessed a huge, open atrium in its middle, each story showcasing something new.

"Most of the levels are filled with dwellings and shopping stalls. Some of the levels contain naught but workers. The uppermost level, for example, is the grindstone. 'Tis where I labor, pounding raw metals into usable materials."

Madalyn wasn't certain if she was supposed to respond. "I see."

Otar pulled the lever up and the elevator came to a jarring stop. "Come," he instructed. "This level has a good view."

She warily followed, wondering what she was about to see. He led her toward a sturdy wall that had been fashioned from dark brown bricks. Once there, he motioned toward it.

"You can see much of the colony from here," he announced. "Come and see it."

Curious, she did just that. Peering over the ledge, her gaze flicked down. "My God," she said quietly.

His world was much bigger than she'd originally thought. Glancing down the atrium, she couldn't even see the lower floors. The levels went on and on, hundreds of them, maybe more. They were up so high that the lower you looked, the more the atrium seemed to narrow, resembling a bottomless pit.

Dizzy, she backed up, feeling disoriented. This was unreal. How could such a vast place exist with nobody above the ground any the wiser?

Because they kill anyone who finds it.

She swallowed hard. Suddenly his obsession with the camera made sense. Otar wouldn't relent until Drake's digital was destroyed. He couldn't. Too much was at stake, not just for him, but for everyone who lived down here.

"This colony is called Lokitown, the capital seat of New Sweden. There are many more such colonies, some of them built like this one, some of them not."

There were *more?* All of them underneath the ground? Unbelievable.

"The Viking world consists of New Sweden, New Norway, and New Daneland. Our ancestors abandoned the Old World above the ground and carved out this new one mayhap as far back as two thousand years ago. Leastways, our written records only go back for one thousand years, so many believe 'tis but that old."

Madalyn blinked. She looked over at Otar. "Why?" She shook her head. "I don't understand why you don't live up there with everyone else."

"We do not care for your ways. Nor will we follow unholy laws. The Vikings listen to none but the gods in Valhalla," he said proudly. "We thrive because we have remained true to the decrees of the gods."

Whether polytheistic or monotheistic, a religious zealot was a religious zealot. She knew there would be no talking him out of his beliefs, so there was no point in arguing them. "I see," she said simply.

His dark eyes searched hers. "One day you will believe," he murmured.

She doubted that but said nothing.

He continued his history lesson. Our ancestors took to living belowground after the prophets warned them of what would happen aboveground."

"And that is?"

"Men tampering with what only the gods have the right to decide. If the prophecies are to be believed, we will see this transpire in our lifetime."

Her forehead wrinkled. "I don't understand what you're trying to say."

"A day will come," he said softly, "when the wenches who live aboveground will die out in numbers. Entire lineages will become extinct. Only below the ground are we safe, for down here we remain true to the gods."

Madalyn frowned. "Our men will not kill us off. That is totally preposterous!"

"Maybe not directly. The gods did not warn the prophets of how the phenomenon would occur, only that it would."

She couldn't believe that an entire race of people existed belowground because of what long-dead prophets had said.

Then again, there were millions of people above the ground who lived out their lives in accordance with their religious beliefs.

A chill slowly worked down her spine. In that moment, all hope of escape dashed. Nobody from her world had ever found this place, because nobody from this world ever let escape happen.

"I want to go home," she said calmly. She glanced away and her breath caught in the back of her throat. "I don't like it here and I never will. It's too different from my world."

"Madalyn . . ."

She stared down the atrium but saw nothing. Her mind was in turmoil, her heart aching. "You will never let me leave here," she whispered. "Will you?"

Silence.

"Tell me the truth."

Otar sighed. "Nay. You cannot leave, Madalyn, and I think you already know that."

Her teeth sank into her bottom lip.

"Lokitown is different from what you are accustomed to, yet I am certain you will thrive here. 'Twill take time to settle into the way of things, but you will."

Madalyn closed her eyes against the damning words. "What will become of me here?" Her eyes flicked open and sought his out. "I'm afraid to ask," she said shakily, "but I need to know."

His face was compassionate but unyielding. "You will become my bride this eve."

Her heartbeat went into overdrive. Adrenaline coursed through her blood so quickly that nausea engulfed her.

"I won't marry you," she said nervously. "I don't even know you."

"We've the rest of our lives for that."

Madalyn's hand flew up to her mouth. She balled it into a fist and sank her teeth into it. Angry and scared, she was also completely powerless. Unbidden, a single tear spilled down her cheek.

"I'm not so bad as that, little one," he murmured as he brushed away the rogue tear. "In time, you will grow to love me."

She pushed his hand away. "I will never love you. Never! And I refuse to marry you! Are you insane? Do you honestly believe I would agree to marry a man who kidnapped me?"

"In my world, your agreement is not necessary."

Her green eyes widened.

There was a hardness in his eyes. "You gave me no choice but to capture you, wench. Did you not take those pictures of me and my men, I would have let you go."

"We weren't taking pictures of you! We were taking them of the whales."

"And we are in them."

That was true and she couldn't deny it. "And if I got you the camera?" Madalyn asked, hope soaring. Maybe she still had a shot at freedom if she handed the wretched thing over to him.

"You still would not be able to leave. 'Tis the law here whether you have a care for it or not."

Her heart sank yet again.

"'Tis sorry I am," Otar murmured. "Leaving is out of the question. Did I attempt to let you go aboveground, I would be branded a heretic and my entire family killed."

"Good grief." She blinked, curious about the rest of what he'd said. "You already have a family?" She frowned. "Do you have other wives?"

He had the nerve to look amused. "Nay. The only family I possess is a mother and twin sister. My sire has been dead to us for ten years and five now."

"Oh. Sorry."

Madalyn ran a hand through her long curly hair and sighed. She didn't know what to do. The only thing she did know was that she didn't want to be married to someone by force. All of her life, she had waited for Mr. Right. Unlike most actresses of her acquaintance, she had never taken the matrimonial plunge. Not one for divorce, she had preferred to stay single until she knew she'd found the right one. There had been occasional whispers in the tabloids that she was a lesbian, because of her longtime single status, but she hadn't cared what people thought.

"Look," Madalyn said. "It's not that you're so bad, and you're very handsome. For a kidnapper."

Again, the amusement. It made him look even more handsome than he already was. A fact she didn't care for in the slightest.

"But I can't marry someone I don't know! I believe marriage is sacred and should be taken seriously. Something done with the love of your life, for the rest of your life."

"As do I," he said softly. "You will grow to love me, Madalyn. Never doubt it."

She shook her head in frustration. "Are you always this arrogant?"

"Aye."

She snorted. "At least you're honest."

"I am."

She turned her back on Otar and looked down the atrium. "So what's the alternative?"

"Your pardon?"

She turned back to him and her jaw tightened. "What other choice do I have here but to marry you? Or do I not have a choice at all?"

"Nay. Under the current jarl, Toki, wenches have no say in their fates."

"Doesn't that just figure."

"I captured you and I am not yet wed. This gives me the right to marry you should I so choose to. 'Tis called Hunter's Right. The only legal way to not become my bride at this juncture is if I choose not to exercise my Hunter's Right."

"And if you choose not to marry me . . . what happens to me then?"

Otar studied her face for a lingering moment before inclining his head. "Come with me and I'll show you."

Chapter Twelve

Otar led Madalyn toward the bride auction block so she would understand that marrying him was not the worst fate she could have.

He was disappointed that she did not already want him, but realistically, all new brides went through the same emotions that Madalyn was experiencing. Inevitably they grew to love their masters, so long as they were properly cared for. Madalyn would be no exception. This he knew.

Still, Otar couldn't help but feel a bit grim about the situation. 'Twas mayhap because she'd been the object of his every fantasy for years, but until yestereve she hadn't even known he existed. As a consequence, she wanted naught to do with him.

Hating him had not been a part of his numerous imaginings about her. Were she any wench but Madalyn, he doubted he'd care so mightily.

"Take my hand before we ascend this stairwell," Otar instructed his captive. "You will want the men you are about to see to know you are mine." When she looked at him skeptically, he said, "If you never believe anything else I say to you, believe this one thing."

She hesitated but took his hand. "Okay." Looking nervous all of a sudden, she added, "You make it sound as though the men are all a bunch of demons or something. Like we'll walk in there and they'll all chase me down while frothing at the mouth."

"Hmmm . . . sort of like those demons that the wench Fanny Fairchild faced whilst trekking over the sea to another land?"

Madalyn stilled and her eyes widened like a kitten's. Gods, she was beautiful. Even more captivating in person than she was in the moving pictures.

"You saw *Attack of the Possessed Pirates?*" she asked, amazed.

"Aye. 'Tis a good one."

She couldn't seem to shake her amazement. "No kidding." She bit her lip. "You really did know who I was when you captured me."

Otar started up the stairwell with her hand in his. "Not until I had you in my arms." He looked down at her and winked. "'Twas an added boon when I saw just who I was obligated to take back to the Underground with me."

She blushed and glanced away. "So what's your favorite movie of mine?"

"I have two. *Song of the Viking* is one, of course." He squeezed her hand. "Victoria falls in love with Thor even though she rages against loving him."

Her blush grew deeper. "What's your other favorite movie?" she hurriedly asked.

"'Twas a saga about a beauty named Gretta who fell in love with a man who disposed of rubbish for his wages."

Madalyn nodded. "Ah, *For the Love of a Garbage Man*." She sighed. "A compelling manuscript, but the guy who played the hero, Howie, was a raging alcoholic."

"Aye?"

"Aye—I mean yes."

She was quiet for a moment as she continued ascending the many steps of the stairwell. Otar found himself wondering what she was thinking.

"I don't get it," Madalyn finally said.

"What do you not understand?"

Having reached the top of the stairwell, Otar walked a few more steps, then turned to face her. He itched to run his hands through that silky, golden-red mane of hers, preferably whilst plowing into her body. For as long as he lived, he would never tire of looking at her. Big green eyes, long curly hair, and skin like cream that possessed nary a blemish.

"I mean, most people tend to like a certain type of movie.

People who enjoy my historical roles, like Victoria in *Song of the Viking,* tend to like my other historical movies. People who like my contemporary roles, such as Gretta in *For the Love of a Garbage Man,* tend to like my other contemporary movies." Her nose wrinkled. "So why those two movies in particular?"

His dark gaze went down to her breasts, then back up to her face. Without using words, he reminded her that those were the two moving pictures she'd bared her sexy, big breasts in.

"Never mind," Madalyn muttered.

Enjoying their back-and-forth banter, Otar hated to bring an end to it. The auction would begin anon, though, and she needed to see it.

"Come," Otar instructed her. "I've something to show you."

"OH MY GOD," Madalyn whispered. Her voice caught in the back of her throat. "This is disgusting."

Of all the things she'd been subjected to since encountering Otar and his men, the bride auction was hands down the worst. Luckily, the only women permitted in the arena proper were the ones being sold. Madalyn and Otar watched from a balcony where the only men remotely close to them were the pitiful few that were too poor to afford a bride.

The arena was huge, an endless sea of male faces. It brought to mind an ancient Roman coliseum, the main difference being that the stage was at a higher elevation than the audience.

Her heart wrenched for the terrified, crying Inuit girl up on stage. Naked and oiled down, she had been restrained so that potential buyers could fondle her. Even from this far away, Madalyn could see the girl shaking.

This was the third woman she'd witnessed get auctioned off. Watching the first two had been difficult enough, and those women hadn't even seemed to mind their fates. Otar had explained that they were natives of New Sweden, so had grown up all of their lives preparing for this day. Indeed, those girls relished the attention, preening more with every whistle and catcall.

Not this girl. Like Madalyn, she was a captive. Otar informed her that the female currently being sold had been the prey of a bride-hunter, a man who makes his living ensnaring women above the ground to sell them to bidders down here.

"You may approach the chattel according to rank," she heard the auctioneer cry out. "My lords, you have first inspection and bidding rights. Proceed!"

Madalyn turned away, unable to watch what she knew was coming next. "I've seen enough," she rasped out. "Please take me away from here."

Thankfully, Otar did as she requested. He couldn't have whisked her out of the arena fast enough to suit her.

"So," Madalyn said as they walked, no doubt sounding as dazed as she felt, "those are my two choices? Marry you or end up on that auction block?"

"Aye." He sighed. "I realize you do not have a care for marrying me, but those are the only two choices either of us possess in regards to your fate. Worse, if I do not take you as my bride within the fortnight, all claims to Hunter's Right are gone."

"So when's the wedding?"

"The what-ing?"

"Wedding. Marriage. When do we get married?"

He snorted. "Ah. Suddenly I am not so bad, eh? 'Tis not the reception I was hoping for, but 'tis a beginning."

Madalyn supposed she could have accepted his desire to marry her with a little more elegance. "I'm sorry," she said sincerely. "I really don't mean to hurt your feelings, but look at things from my perspective."

"I am. Which is why I do not let your words hurt me."

He was lying. She didn't know how she knew, but she was as certain of that fact as she was that her name was Madalyn Mae Simon. She snuck a glance at his face as they walked. She had never expected to see even a lick of vulnerability in him and didn't know what to make of it.

"So how do we get married here?" Madalyn asked, curious.

Otar came to a halt and faced her. "Are you ready?"

She straightened her back, her chin notching up. "I am."

"You needn't look like you're preparing yourself for the gallows."

The twinkle was back in his eyes. She swallowed as she realized she preferred it there—just because it was far less frightening than his anger, of course.

"I'm an actress. We tend to be a touch dramatic," she sniffed.

"And your sister? She's an actress, too?"

Madalyn waved that notion away. "She's just paranoid. She believes the government is responsible for every bad thing that happens."

"Are they?"

"I don't know. I don't think about it."

Otar scratched his chin as he gazed down at Madalyn. "Does she believe our people to be of this government, then?"

"No, she thinks you're aliens. You know, creatures from another planet."

"I see."

"Look," Madalyn said, coming to the point, "I don't want to end up naked on that auction block. I'd rather marry you."

"Thank you. I think."

Her face colored. "I didn't mean it like that."

His gaze found hers. "Aye, you did, but I'll take what I can for now."

Otar reached out and took her hands in his. Butterflies swarmed in her stomach despite herself.

"Madalyn . . ."

"Yes?"

"I declare Hunter's Right."

"Okay. So when are we getting married?"

Otar blinked. "I just married us. 'Tis all I had to say. You are mine now."

"That's it?" She frowned. "How anticlimactic."

It took her a moment to absorb the fullness of the situation. "We're really married now?"

"Aye."

The way he said "aye" snagged her full attention. It had come out in a hoarse voice, accompanied by eyelids so heavy he looked drugged. She knew he was more than eager to consummate the marriage.

"Let us go," Otar commanded, snapping out of it. "'Tis time for you to see your new home."

Chapter Thirteen

His cock was so hard it ached. Had Otar taken a native of New Sweden to wife, she would have expected to consummate their marriage the same eve. He realized he would have to be patient with Madalyn. Unfortunately and ironically, she was the only woman alive he knew he'd have trouble staying away from.

The elevator came to a jarring stop at sector 75. Otar blew out a breath as he pushed the lever up, securing it into place. Opening the cage, he motioned for his wife to follow him.

His wife. He'd spent all these years pumping his shaft with his hand, his thoughts of Madalyn, but never had he imagined he'd actually possess her. She was legally his now. No other man could ever touch her. No other man would ever dare try.

Jarl or no, not even Toki could gainsay the sacred laws of marriage. Did he so much as look at Madalyn lustfully, 'twould be Otar's right as a husband to challenge him to fight to the death. His cousin would never be so foolish as that.

Otar's muscles tensed up as they neared the enclave of tiny, run-down homes where his family, and several other families, dwelled. Madalyn deserved so much more than this and he wanted to give it to her. With Toki in power, 'twould never happen. Now that Madalyn was his wife, he was even more eager for the Revolution to begin.

His bastard cousin had reinstituted an old law that no jarl had recognized in over five hundred years as his means to legally oust the Thordssons from their world of privilege. While Toki possessed no means by which he could strip the paternal side of his family of all aristocratic rights, he was able to maneuver the nobles, most of whom were terrified of his wrath, to recognize the disenfranchisement of the maternal side. The paternal side carried Toki's surname, the maternal side didn't. 'Twas as simple, and ridiculous, as that.

All these years later, Otar's nostrils still flared every time he recalled the look of anguish on his mother's face the day their home was confiscated. She had lived in that dwelling all of her life. As her sire's only heir, the familial home had been gifted to her upon his death. 'Twas the only memory of her sire she had to hold on to. Now she didn't even have that.

"Our home is this way," Otar informed Madalyn. "Toward the back."

Leading her between a cluster of ramshackle dwellings, he found himself embarrassed to bring her here. He had worked so hard all of his life, yet Toki's law forbade him to buy property outside of Shanty Row.

The people of Shanty Row were good and kind, their only crime being poverty. Because sturdy materials to craft dwellings with were expensive in New Sweden, the lowest of the laboring class had to make do with scraps that had been left over. As a result, their homes were forever rotting. The males of the village regularly pitched in and helped each other patch up their dwellings, but 'twas only so much men could do with the pitiful scraps of bark and mud they had to work with.

Otar took Madalyn by the hand as they walked through a dirt-packed alleyway. They passed by a small cantina where Shanty Rowers regularly came together for food, drink, and laughs. He smiled at a group of people he knew as they jovially called out to him, but waved away their invitation to sit.

"Are those your friends?" Madalyn asked.

"Aye."

"I don't mind if you want to stop and talk to them."

Very generous of her, but if he stopped at the cantina before introducing his new bride to his family, his mother would be aggrieved. Worse, she would harangue him over the slight for years to come.

"We can stop here and eat another time," Otar responded. "This eve you must meet my mother and sister."

He could tell she was getting nervous from the way she chewed on her lower lip. 'Twas a decidedly adorable habit. "Why?"

His eyebrows shot up. "You are my wife. They will want to know you."

"I see."

"'Tis no need to be scared, Madalyn. They will not bite you if you're nice to them," he teased.

"This is all so much to take in," she said quietly. "I'd really just like to eat something and go to sleep."

Otar realized she wanted to go to sleep without him, but such would not occur. He would not force her into sex this eve, but he wanted her to grow accustomed to his presence in their bed.

"We will," he murmured, getting hard just thinking about how small the bed was. For once there was a boon in not being permitted to own luxuries such as large beds. "Very soon."

WALKING DOWN THE CRUDE ALLEYWAY, Madalyn was intrigued by the mud-and-twig homes nestled every which way. For a holiday, dwelling in this cute, quaint place would be a blast, but for evermore? Her heart sank at the thought of never being able to go above the ground again.

All that she knew, everything she'd taken for granted her entire life, was lost to her. The thought of never laying eyes on her ancestral home in Alabama was hard to bear. The fear that she would be separated from Drake for even another day brought tears to her eyes.

Clichéd as it sounded, she truly didn't know what she'd had until it was gone. The places, she could live without, but the people, namely her little sister . . . never.

Madalyn noticed that the farther they walked, the grimmer Otar's mood became. She wasn't sure what had brought the change over him, but it made her uncomfortable.

"Which house is yours?" she asked, hoping to engage him in conversation.

"We're almost there," he muttered. "It looks just like the rest of them. If you've seen one, you've seen them all."

"The homes here are very cute. You must love living here."

Otar came to a sudden halt. Releasing her hand, he turned around to face her. The anger and accusation on his face made her heart race. Her eyes widened, having no idea what she'd done wrong.

"Do not tell me lies," he hissed. "I understand that you do not wish to be my wife. I desire for your feelings to be otherwise, but I can tolerate them for what they are. What I can never abide are lies." His nostrils flared, scaring Madalyn. "Do not tell one again."

"I-I wasn't lying," she breathed out. Dumbfounded, she didn't understand what had brought on his 180-degree change in mood. "I really think the homes here are cute. They remind me of the kind of little huts my people vacation in while in Tahiti and tropical places like that. Granted, I've never seen such a home in a polar region, but down here I've seen a lot of things I never knew existed."

His expression slowly softened, and he studied her face for a lingering moment before speaking.

"I should not have yelled at you." Otar ran a hand over his jaw and sighed. "This place . . ." Frowning, he glanced around and shook his head. "'Tis a sore subject for me. You have my apologies, Madalyn."

"It's okay," she whispered. "We've all got sore points. Couldn't be human without them."

"You have a forgiving nature," he murmured, his gaze searching hers. "'Tis a beautiful quality."

She blushed and glanced away. "Thank you."

He took her hand in his again and continued walking. "In your world, people really like wee stick-and-mud homes such as these?"

"Yeah. They pay big money to vacation in them."

"Your people are strange to me."

Madalyn snorted at that. "Your people aren't exactly what *I'd* call normal."

"Touché."

"Buying and selling women, kidnapping people, living below the ground . . . this would make for a great horror movie."

Otar laughed, an infectious sound that made her smile

despite herself. She didn't want to warm up to the guy, since she still dreamed of escaping, but he made the task of not liking him difficult. "'Twould make an interesting saga. Mayhap more interesting than *Song of the Viking.*"

She smiled as they continued walking. More men shouted out their hellos as they passed by, and it dawned on Madalyn that she had yet to see a female in this area. Why?

"We are here," Otar told her, pointing to the tiny house in front of them. "'Tis time to meet my family."

For some insane reason, Madalyn hoped they liked her. Nervous, she inclined her head. "Let's go in, then."

Chapter Fourteen

Her body tense, Madalyn entered the twig-and-clay home behind Otar. Once inside, he walked over to a nearby door. Rapping on it, he called out to his family in their language. Madalyn couldn't help but visually inspect the place while they stood there and waited.

Otar's home was a paradox of austerity and comfort. While minuscule and lacking decoration, it was well kept and managed to appear homey. On the far right side of the room, white polar bear furs draped the bed. A matching animal skin served as a rug on the floor. A small kitchen sat in the middle of the dirt-floored hut, and a table and four chairs were situated at the far left of it, next to the door Otar had pounded on when announcing their arrival.

"My mother and twin sister live in an adjoining dwelling," he explained. "They are expecting us and will make their appearances anon."

"All right." A curious expression in her gaze, she looked up at him. "If the door on the far left leads to your mother and sister's house, then where does that door lead?" she asked, pointing to a frame of wood opposite where she stood.

"'Tis a bathing chamber," he informed her. "We share it with my mother and sister. Leastways, we are fortunate to share with none but them; many in Shanty Row must share with four or five other families."

Considering the alternative, Madalyn had to agree that sharing with only three other people was a good thing. Growing up, her family of four had shared one bathroom, so she could adjust for the time being. No matter what surprises lay ahead, she needed to keep things in perspective: she planned to leave, so this didn't matter.

The door to the left opened, startling Madalyn. Teeth sinking into her bottom lip, she darted her gaze toward the two women entering the house.

Otar and his twin sister must have inherited their height and dark good looks from their father, for their mother, while quite beautiful herself, was a diminutive blonde with fair skin. Neither of her children resembled her to a great degree, but their similar bone structures gave away the genetic tie.

Blinking several times, Madalyn couldn't believe how they were dressed. Both, regardless of age, brought to mind

Playboy bunnies, women who dressed for the pleasure of men.

They wore long, sleeveless garments that started just above the bosom and draped to the ankles; and their breasts were thrust up and forward by elastic material that created the effect of an empire waist. That by itself would have been tolerable; the fact that the garments were so sheer as to cause Madalyn to blush was not. The mother wore a blue dress, the sister a green one. Their nipples, overly evident, stabbed against the sheer fabric, leaving little to the imagination.

Hysterically wondering if there was a chance in hell that these Viking people had discovered the wonder that is the piña colada, she hoped with everything she had in her that Otar didn't expect her to dress like that. She'd feel like an idiot! Not to mention a raging slut.

She had seen other females similarly clothed when she'd first arrived, but everything had been too new, too surreal, to absorb it at the time. Now the nuances of life below the earth were starting to sink in and take root.

Her gaze landing on Madalyn, Otar's mother's eyes lit up and sparkled a brilliant blue. "She is quite beautiful," the matriarch said, smiling. She glanced up at her son before looking back to Madalyn. "You have done well, my son. A lovely wife she is indeed."

Wife. Madalyn was still shocked to hear someone refer to her as any man's wife.

Is this what is happening to Drake? Is she meeting Iiro's family this very moment and feeling as freaked out as I am?

A bemused expression stole over Madalyn's face. If Iiro

had married her sister, she would give anything to be a fly on the wall when he took his angry bride home to meet his family. She'd accuse them all of being aliens and government sympathizers within five minutes.

"'Tis an honor to have you join our family," Otar's twin sister pronounced, snagging Madalyn's attention. Her smile was genuine, kind. "I feared my brother would never take a wife. 'Tis a joy to know our line will continue through you."

Uncertain what to say, Madalyn guessed that admitting she planned to escape before a baby was conceived wouldn't be the ideal response. "Thank you," she said, smiling politely back. "That's very kind of you."

"Madalyn," Otar thankfully interrupted, coming to stand next to her. "I would like you to make the acquaintance of my mother, Annikki, and my sister, Agata. Mama, Agata, this is Madalyn."

"A beautiful name," Annikki chimed in. "To match a beautiful face."

"Aye," Agata agreed, "though her clothes are strange to me."

Madalyn's gaze darted down her body, inspecting herself. Well if that wasn't the pot calling the kettle black! Her khakis were unattractive, but at least they covered her important parts.

"Come," Annikki instructed them, "let us sit down to eat. My daughter and I have prepared a delicious meal."

Madalyn followed them to the small table and sank down into a chair.

Over the next hour, she found that she sincerely liked both Annikki and Agata. Cheerful and humorous, they both managed to squeeze laughs out of her, something she'd thought impossible.

It was easy to see that Otar dearly loved his family. She'd rarely seen him smile since the moment he'd captured her, but he did so easily in their presence. They were closely knit, the essence of what a family was supposed to be. It was a rare phenomenon in Madalyn's Hollywood world, something she hadn't experienced since her mom and dad had died.

Growing up, Madalyn and Drake hadn't possessed much in the way of material things, but oh how they had been loved. A part of her wondered if both of them had remained single so long because deep down inside they had realized neither one of them would be able to recapture the love and devotion they had known in their childhood.

She studied Otar's face. His attention was hitched by a story Agata was telling, and Madalyn could watch him without him knowing it. She found herself thinking what a handsome, strong man he was . . . and wishing she would have met him under far different circumstances.

She drew in a breath and slowly, quietly exhaled. There was no point in denying that she was attracted to Otar, whether she wanted to be or not. He possessed a solid, dependable, loyal presence that was hard not to admire. She instinctively understood that he'd never let anyone down here harm her. It was hard not to warm up to qualities such as those.

Blinking, she frowned, deciding she was suffering from Stockholm syndrome. It simply wasn't reasonable for a victim to start liking her captor, let alone find him attractive.

"You look fatigued," Agata said to Madalyn. She threw a long, silky lock of black hair over her shoulder. "'Tis been a long day for you, aye?"

"Yes," she said quietly. "It has."

"Let us go, so you can rest." Annikki stood up and motioned for her daughter to follow. "We will see you on the morrow, Madalyn. Thank you, again, for joining our family."

"Do you need anything whilst Otar is not about, you have but to knock on the door to summon us," Agata added with a smile. "We are always nearby."

"I'll remember that. Thank you."

Standing up, Madalyn accepted their embraces. Stiff at first, her muscles slowly softened as Annikki and then Agata hugged her.

"On the morrow, son," Annikki said in the way of goodbye, giving Otar her cheek to kiss.

"On the morrow, Mama," he murmured back.

When they were gone, the door firmly shut behind them, Madalyn found herself wishing them back. Stupid as it sounded, she hadn't considered the fact that once they left, Otar might want to consummate their marriage.

Their eyes met and locked. She nervously nibbled on her lower lip as his brooding gaze raked over her.

"You look as fatigued as Agata insisted you were," Otar said.

"I am."

"I should like for you to rest, then."

Madalyn gave a none-too-subtle sigh of relief. She didn't know what to make of the amusement in his eyes. "I think I should now."

Otar nodded. "I agree. But first there is something you must do for me. Two things, actually."

Her gaze warily searched his. "What's the first one?"

His expression was hard, unwavering. "You must give me the picture-taker."

"Picture-taker? Oh, you mean the camera?" She splayed her hands. "I told you I don't have it. I'm not lying."

"Mayhap you are not, yet is there only one way for me to be certain. This proof is the second thing you must do for me."

Something told her she wouldn't like this. "What?"

His gaze flicked down to her breasts, then back up to her face. "Take off your clothes," he ordered her. "All of them."

Chapter Fifteen

Madalyn's heart was beating so fast, she thought she might faint. "What?" she squeaked. "I-I don't think I heard you correctly."

"You heard me properly. Do it, Madalyn, lest I do it for you."

Had she begun to think he was at all attractive? That he possessed some admirable qualities? Well, he wasn't and he didn't, she thought, angry. She had never been so humiliated in her entire life. With twelve years of acting under her belt, that was saying a lot.

"You bastard!" she yelled, her face bright with fury. "If you're going to rape me, just get it over with. You don't need to play mind games with me!"

His expression turned impossibly harder. "I will not rape you, Madalyn. I *will* know that you do not possess the camera, in which case your sister will be searched."

Oh . . . no. She couldn't stand the thought of her baby sister being dragged through such a humiliating ordeal.

"She doesn't have the camera, either! I swear it. It's back at my cabin."

"Your cabin was searched, Madalyn. 'Twas not there."

Realizing there were no choices left to her, she closed her eyes briefly and sighed.

"It's hidden," she told him. "The camera is underneath the floorboards where my jewels are also kept."

He was quiet for a prolonged moment, and then said, "Take off your clothes, Madalyn. As your husband and master, I command you to do so."

Husband and *master?*

"I am not, nor will I ever be," she said harshly, "any man's slave."

"I would expect no less."

Confused, she decided that *master* must mean something else down here.

"As your husband," Otar informed her, "I am your master. I make your decisions, I tell you where you may go, who you may go with, and how long you are permitted to be gone. 'Tis the way of it since the beginning of my people's history."

Madalyn frowned. No, the word *master* did not have a different meaning down here.

Too emotionally exhausted to argue, Madalyn ran a hand through her mane of hair and sighed.

"I want to go to sleep," she whispered, her expression pleading. "I'm begging you to let me."

"I will not breach you, Madalyn. Leastways, not this eve. Do as you've been bade and I will permit you to slumber."

She would get what she wanted, but she would pay his price. Staring at him like this, their gazes fixed in challenge, she realized he would never relent. She could kick and scream, curse and rile against him, but in the end it wouldn't change a blessed thing.

If nothing else could be said in the way of virtue about Otar, he *was* a man of his word. He had said he wouldn't rape her, and she knew she could believe him.

Going down on her knees to the dirt floor, Madalyn untied one boot and then the other, fumbling with the laces. "For the record, I have never been treated so horribly in my entire life."

"I do not wish to hurt you, Madalyn. 'Tis sorry I am that you hate me so."

"I don't hate you," she admitted, standing up and kicking her boots over to him for inspection. "But that doesn't change the fact that I will never be happy here."

His gaze flicked over her face. "Time changes many things, little one. You will grow to love me one day. I vow it."

Madalyn didn't know what to say to that, so she said nothing. Leaning against the kitchen table, she pulled off her socks one at a time, then threw them at his feet.

"Very good," he said, studying the boots and socks and finding nothing amiss. His voice lowered, grew thicker. "Now remove the rest of your clothing."

She stilled. Glancing down the length of his body, the sight of his erection unnerved her. Otar did nothing to conceal it, nor did he attempt to apologize for it. But then, neither did he make a move to do anything about it.

"All right." Madalyn's fingers reached for the hem of her Army-green T-shirt. Grabbing it with both hands, she pulled it over her head and flung it at him. A crimson bra was the only thing shielding her upper body from his total view.

He sucked in his breath.

Madalyn unzipped the khakis next and slithered out of them, revealing panties that matched her bra. His erection grew bigger against his black pants. Nervously throwing the khakis at Otar, she saw how heavy-lidded his gaze was becoming.

"And the rest," he said hoarsely, his eyes smoldering with intensity.

Madalyn reached around and unclasped her bra, then she tugged at the straps and jiggled out of it.

Straightening her back, she stood before her captor topless. Her large breasts were completely revealed, her pink nipples firm. As she looked into Otar's eyes, she saw unadulterated lust. All of her senses were alert, her belly in knots.

"You have beautiful nipples," he said, his voice thick. "I've dreamt of kissing and suckling them for years."

For some insane reason, his words made her nipples

stiffen up. Embarrassed, she reached for her panties. Securing a string in either hand, Madalyn pushed the panties down, wiggling them to her feet and kicking them away from her.

Otar's gaze honed in on her most intimate, private area. Perspiration broke out on his forehead. "You are golden red all over," he murmured.

Against her volition, her body began to respond to his arousal. Not only were her nipples as hard as rocks, she could also feel dampness between her legs. She squeezed her thighs together.

Have you lost what's left of your mind, Madalyn Mae Simon? You don't get wet when the man who kidnapped you stares at your naked body!

Her heart beat faster and faster, her breasts rose up and down in time with her labored breathing.

"I told you I didn't have the camera," she said, wanting to break the tense hush that had ensorcelled the hut. "I didn't lie."

The silence continued. Madalyn's gaze flicked up to meet Otar's face. Her breathing grew worse.

Never, not once in all of her life, had a man stared at her with the passion Otar was staring at her with now. She'd never seen a man so aroused, so eager and wanting her. During her acting career, Madalyn had been coveted by more than a few groupies, but none of them had looked at her like *this*. She couldn't even define what *this* was . . . she just knew it was a vastly different experience than what she was accustomed to.

If it wasn't too stupid of a notion to entertain, she would have wondered if that was love she saw in his eyes. But that was impossible, she told herself. Nobody can love someone in just a day.

"Nay," Otar huskily admitted, blinking to regain control of his mind, "you did not lie. 'Tis an admirable quality for a wife to possess."

"May I go to sleep now?" she asked unsteadily. "I'm very tired."

Otar's muscles corded with the effort not to take her right here and now. The desire to pick her up, carry her to their bed, and fuck her until he was nigh unto dead was powerfully consuming. He wanted to mount her more than he wanted to breathe.

He had given her his word that he would not consummate their marriage this eve, and he intended to keep it. But, he told himself as he slowly reached down and ran his fingers through her downy hair, he had said nothing of touching her.

Madalyn tensed up and opened her mouth to speak, but he forestalled her.

"Shhh," Otar said softly, his middle finger finding her clit and gently rubbing it, "I told you I will not make love to you this eve and I will not."

Her eyelids grew heavy as she looked at him through a semiworried, semidrugged gaze. "Then why are you touching me like this?" she gasped.

His jaw tightened. "I want you to grow accustomed to

me. 'Twill make the consummation much easier on you when it occurs."

'Twas true, mayhap, yet it wasn't the reason he was touching her. He touched her because he couldn't stand not to. Here she was in his arms, the woman he had spent years coveting. He praised the gods for guiding him to Madalyn.

Otar picked up the pace, massaging her clit in a firm, circular motion. His cock nigh unto exploded as he watched Madalyn gaze at him through lustful eyes. The sound of her moans and the feel of her drenched pussy made him so hard as to be painful.

"Come for me," Otar murmured, mesmerized by her carnal expression. He gently pushed her down onto the table. "Come for your husband, Madalyn."

She arched her back, causing her breasts to thrust up. Splaying her thighs wide, his gorgeous wife moaned and groaned as he rubbed her. Replacing his hand with his mouth, he greedily dove for her flesh and sucked it hard.

"Oh God. Otar—what are you—*oh God.*"

Her body began to convulse, and he knew that she was coming. He sucked on her clit harder, wanting to bring her over the edge.

"*Ooooohhhhhh!*" she screamed, unable to hold back the rush. "*Ohhhhh Godddddd!*"

Madalyn came on a wail, giving him her juice. He lapped at her like a boy with a favored treat, savoring every nuance of her orgasm. The way she looked, the way she sounded, her intoxicating, tangy scent . . .

Otar slowly lifted his head from between his wife's legs. Her breathing was heavy, her eyes round as moons. Clearly, she was confused by her feelings. 'Twas normal for a new bride, so he didn't dwell on it.

"You taste delicious," he told Madalyn, helping her up from the table. "'Tis almost time to sleep."

"A-almost?" she stammered.

"Aye," he said softly. "Almost."

He picked her up and carried her to their bed.

MADALYN HAD NEVER BEEN MORE BAFFLED by her behavior, or more embarrassed. She had told Otar she would never find happiness here. Having an orgasm for him hardly backed up her words convincingly.

Now he was carrying her to the bed. A bed that was looking more ominous with every passing moment. Could she blame him for trying? If she were a man, wouldn't she try to bed someone who'd just climaxed in her presence less than a minute ago?

She had never been big on one-night stands. As a result, sex tended to make her feel closer to a man. And the last thing she needed was to feel closer to Otar. It would only serve to convolute an already murky relationship.

He sat her on the bed. Standing over her, all muscles and erection, he looked even more powerful. She reached for a fur on the bed behind her and quickly draped it over her front.

"Otar . . ."

"I told you we will not consummate this eve, Madalyn. I will honor my vow to you."

She hesitated. "Then what's going on?"

"We are going to lie in bed. Together." He began to remove his chain-mail tunic.

"What are you doing?" she breathed out.

Sweet lord, his body was ruthless in its strength. She had known he was heavily muscled, but seeing those muscles up close and personal, no clothing to impede the view, was overwhelming. His chest was solid and impressively delineated, his nipples dark and flat. Black hair sprinkled his chest before tapering into a thin line and disappearing into his animal-hide pants.

She'd never seen a man built like Otar. He didn't have the overly bulky build of the steroid junkies that frequented L.A.'s posh gyms, but the honed, deadly physique of a warrior who could kill you with his bare hands.

"In my world, husbands and wives sleep together," Otar told her. He looked at her pointedly as he stepped out of his boots and then proceeded to undo his pants. "Naked."

She blinked, having momentarily forgotten the thread of the conversation. "I'm not from this world," she weakly protested, realizing he was unlikely to cave in.

"Aye, you are. Leastways, now you are."

Madalyn watched with a little too much fascination as he pushed his pants down. She swallowed when his erection sprang free, immediately noting how long and thick it was. Rising up from a nest of dark curls, it looked more than eager and willing to hurry the consummation along.

"I guess it's true what they say about the size of a man's hands," Madalyn muttered to herself.

"Eh?"

Her cheeks went up in flames. "Never mind."

"Scoot over," Otar murmured. "I will hold you whilst you sleep."

Madalyn worried her lip. The bed was small; there wasn't anywhere to scoot *to*. And she was certain she wouldn't be able to sleep with Otar lying next to her naked.

Her back to Otar, she lay down on her side, her face close to the wall. Otar's heavy weight pressed into the bed beside her, a large, vein-roped arm snaking over her hip. Madalyn thought it was as close as they could get without having sex. She was wrong.

Apparently unhappy that the polar bear fur kept his body from touching hers, Otar slid underneath it and pressed impossibly closer. She could feel his erection poking against her back, hungry to do more than lie there waiting. He draped his arm over her middle again and held her securely.

"You are the most beautiful woman I've ever laid eyes on," he murmured, his right hand nudging her head to his bicep and then tenderly stroking her hair. "Soft and vulnerable, determined and strong." He bent his head and kissed her temple. "You are perfect and you are mine."

Madalyn closed her eyes against his words. They were the sort of heartfelt sentiments she'd hoped to hear from the lips of the man she married one day, but she had never dreamed of things happening in this manner. At war with the woman who she was, the frightened child inside of her couldn't help but snuggle closer, wanting his strength and larger-than-life presence as near as possible.

Her eyes flicked open, her back still to him. "You try to make me feel loved in order to keep me from raging against you," she whispered. "That's not an emotion you should play with."

He stilled. "Madalyn——"

"I've been searching for a man to love me, really love me, all of my life." She felt tears well up in her eyes but refused to shed them. "Romantic love doesn't exist, Otar. It's an illusion, the stuff of books and movies. You can keep up the charade if you'd like, but you're not fooling me."

He rolled her over so he could make eye contact. "'Tis not a game to me. I do love you, and one day soon you will grow to love me in return."

She sighed, shaking her head. She'd been down this road before, though never to such an extent. "It's not me you love, Otar." Her smile was kind and a little sad. "It's Victoria."

He opened his mouth to protest, but she gently placed a finger over his lips. "That's what I meant when I said I've always wanted someone to love *me*—the real me. You fell in love with a role I played, not with the woman I truly am."

His eyes narrowed, but he didn't deny her words. Madalyn knew that he couldn't.

She rolled back over onto her side, determined to fall

asleep. She sighed, her heart heavy. Crazy or not, she actually felt a bit gloomy by his lack of protests.

What do you want him to do, swear that he loves you? Lie to you? Tell you all the words your pathetic little psyche wants to hear? That's why you became an actress, after all. You naively believed that fame equaled love.

Madalyn closed her eyes tightly. She wanted to go to sleep, to forget about the Achilles heel she had just presented Otar with. Love was the only thing lacking in her life . . . and the one thing she craved more than anything else.

To let the very man who'd taken her prisoner in on that secret was akin to idiocy. She didn't want him to know her vulnerabilities, yet she'd just handed the biggest of them over on a silver platter.

She was insane. The situation was insane. Her feelings and behavior toward Otar repeatedly shifted from semi-friendly to obstinate and back again. She needed to be one way and stay that way.

But it was difficult. A part of her liked him as a person, regardless of the situation. Another part of her wanted him to go away so life could go back to normal. Hollywood hadn't been perfect, or even close—but at least she had been free.

Chapter Sixteen

Madalyn awoke the next morning to the sound of loud, angry shouts. She sat up, careful to keep the fur wrapped around her. Immediately recognizing one of the voices as belonging to Otar, it took her a moment to pinpoint the other voice.

Iiro.

Her pulse picking up, she got out of bed and pressed her ear against the wall nearest the front door. She suspected they were discussing Drake, and any news about her sister was welcome.

Listening intently, she gratefully realized they were conversing in English.

"What do you mean she escaped?" Otar bellowed. Madalyn's eyes widened from the other side of the wall. "How could such a thing happen?"

"I don't know, milord," Iiro grumbled, obviously embarrassed. "Leastways, she was there by my side one moment and gone the next."

"Where did this happen?"

"At my sire's dwelling. She disappeared not long after I declared my Hunter's Right."

So he *had* married her. Madalyn found a crack in the wall big enough to peep at them through.

"'Twas an awful consummation," Iiro ground out, pacing. "The sex was good enough to kill a man, but all the events before and after it vexed me to no end."

"You consummated last eve?" Otar asked, sounding as disbelieving as Madalyn was. "She let you do this?"

"Oh, aye." He waved that away. "She all but attacked me. 'Tis the one boon to her otherwise grim disposition."

One side of Madalyn's mouth kicked up in a half-smile.

"I do not follow," Otar grunted. "If she wanted to consummate, why did she run?"

He threw his hands up. "I doubt the gods themselves know what lurks in the mind of my wife!" Exasperated, he listed her many sins. "When first I brought her to my parents' dwelling and declared my Hunter's Right, she informed everyone present that she would be cutting off my man-parts that very eve."

Madalyn snorted. *Go, Drake, go.*

"At evening repast she accused the lot of us of possessing

'too blue eyes'—whatever in Odin that is—and insisted we were aliens from another planet with plans to inhabit her brain."

Madalyn saw Otar hide a smile. He was obviously amused but didn't want to laugh at his friend's expense.

"My mother, Frigg bless her, still attempted to engage Drake in conversation. Even after she forced my sire's jaw open to see if he was possessed of a forked tongue!"

"Forked tongue?"

"Aye. She poked it to make certain 'twas a human's tongue."

"Your wife is bizarre."

Iiro frowned. "'Twas her way of testing him to see if he was an alien. Were my sire an alien, 'twould have been a very crafty thing my wife did."

Madalyn couldn't help but be warmed by the way he was defending her.

"I see."

"With your permission, I should like to go hunt her down on the Outside. Alone. She abandoned me and I've a score to settle with my wench."

"Get the camera whilst you're there."

"Madalyn does not have it?"

"Nay, but she told me where to retrieve it. Beneath the floor of that cottage."

Iiro inclined his head. "'Tis done."

"Do not let your wife escape again," Otar warned. "Now go retrieve her."

Iiro flushed. "Aye, milord." He turned to walk away, then pivoted back to face Otar. "I almost forgot," he said, grinning.

"Aye?"

"We are not the only warriors who declared Hunter's Right last eve. Lord Ericsson did as well."

Otar grunted. "Truth be told, I believed he would."

Madalyn lost interest once the subject turned to people she didn't know. She hurried away from the door and scooted back into the bed. She glanced around for her clothing but didn't see it. When the door creaked open a moment later, she swaddled the polar bear fur tightly around her.

Drake had escaped! Deep down inside, she had doubted such a thing would be possible. Still, Madalyn realized her sister's flight to freedom was far from over. Iiro was as tenacious as Otar—he would never give up.

"You are awake."

"Thank you for stating the obvious."

Otar's eyebrows shot up. "I see we are feeling our old, cranky self again."

"I'm not cranky." She frowned. "I am hungry. I want to eat, but I don't see my clothes."

"You don't need clothes in order to eat."

She sighed. "Otar, I can only handle so many changes at once. I'm not eating naked this morning!"

There was a teasing gleam in his eyes. "We can eat naked at the evening's repast, then."

"You're giving me a headache," she whined, dramatically raising a hand to her forehead. "They should take you into elementary schools to scare the daylights out of the kids. You know, sort of a living testament to the fact that bad things happen to little girls who venture too far from home."

He clucked his tongue as he neared the bed. "I'm not so bad as that, am I?"

"I will answer that question after you give up my clothes."

"I will give you some clothing to don after you give me a good-morn kiss."

Madalyn sighed like a martyr. "You're determined to drive me insane."

"Do insane people harp on their husbands at every given opportunity?"

"Yes! They are much worse!"

"Then I can't have that. Now kiss me good morn."

The more she baited him, the more Otar seemed to enjoy the banter. Unfortunately, he wasn't the only one. Madalyn found herself cracking a small smile.

"You're a goof," she said, exasperated. "Do you know that?"

"If a goof is fair, handsome, and possessed of admirable lovemaking skills, then I must agree."

She suppressed a laugh, and the ensuing sound came out like a snort. "Doesn't anything get to you?"

"You do," Otar admitted, his expression growing serious. "I want to make you the happiest you've ever been, Madalyn."

Her smile faltered. She wanted to shout at him not to say things like that, not to try to make her care about him, but couldn't bring herself to hurt his feelings. "You're a good man," she said. "Your people are twisted and your marrying ways are beyond obscene, but you're a good man."

"Thank you. I think."

Their gazes clashed and held. Nervous, Madalyn wanted to bite her lip. Instead, she closed her eyes and slowly offered her lips to him for a kiss.

Otar's mouth gently covered hers. The kiss was a soft caress, a lingering brush of sensation that did much more toward arousing her than a hard, demanding kiss ever could have. Her breathing growing heavy, she broke away, giving him her profile.

"Thank you for the good-morn kiss," he murmured.

"You're welcome," she said quietly.

She could feel Otar's searing gaze on her, though she didn't look at him. He wanted her. Without a doubt he'd take her this very moment if she showed even the slightest inclination toward being intimate with him.

"I'll get your clothes," Otar said, following a tense silence. "'Tis time to break our fast."

Chapter Seventeen

They weren't the clothes she'd had in mind, but starving, she decided they would do in a pinch. Madalyn quickly got dressed in a sheer green dress and matching sandals. Otar was next door retrieving his mother and sister and she wanted to be fully clothed when they walked in. Or as fully clothed as a woman could be when forced to dress like a raging slut.

"Good morn, daughter," Annikki called out to Madalyn.

Madalyn was taken aback by the term of endearment. No woman had called her daughter since her mom died, and she didn't care for what it did to her heart.

"Good morning." Madalyn inclined her head respectfully. "Did you sleep well?"

"Quite." Annikki embraced her, then kissed her cheek. "You look even lovelier now than you did yestereve. You've shed that garb you called clothes and donned the dress of our women."

Madalyn blinked. Glancing from a bemused Otar and back to a serious Annikki, she borrowed a line from the man who had married her. "Thank you. I think."

Agata chuckled. "Good morn, sister," she said with a smile, before embracing her and kissing her cheek.

"Good morning, Agata."

As Madalyn smelled the food Otar had carried in from his family's adjoining hut, her belly began to rumble.

"Ah," Annikki said, pointing toward a chair. "You are hungry. Let us eat, then."

Madalyn had enjoyed the women's company the night before, and did so again. Annikki and Agata were a hoot. They loved to gossip, both of them telling stories with enough wit to put David Letterman to shame.

The one and only thing that bothered her about the conversation was the fervor with which the Thordsson women recounted the prophesies of their people's ancient seers. Changing their opinions where the dictates of the gods and goddesses of Valhalla were concerned was clearly not an option. They believed that the number of females existing above the ground would die out—and soon. Nothing she said could refute their deeply ingrained beliefs.

The conversation took a turn toward marriage customs, and Madalyn's ears perked up further. To hear Otar's mother tell it, the Viking men had been hunting down women from above the ground for as long as their race had dwelled below it.

Tradition, Annikki called it. Madalyn dourly wondered why their people had chosen kidnapping to be their communal tradition. They should just let off fireworks or have parades like normal people.

"So tell me," Madalyn asked Agata, setting her cup down. "If this marriage auction block is unavoidable, how did you manage to avoid it?"

"'Twas easy," she replied, waving that away. "Shanty Rowers are considered undesirables, thank the gods." She shrugged. "No man would have me."

Though Agata's words had been lighthearted, Madalyn sensed the pain behind them. "I don't understand. You're beautiful."

Agata blushed. "Nay, not really."

"Yes," Madalyn said definitively, "you are." She sat up straighter in her seat, an air of authority stealing over her. "I was an actress. I know beauty when I see it and you, my dear, are every casting director's dream come true."

"I know not what a casting director is, but I thank you for your compliment."

"Why are people who live here considered undesirable?"

Annikki sighed and answered. "'Tis where the poorest of New Sweden dwell."

So, a caste system of sorts. Madalyn's gaze flicked over to Otar, who was studying her intently. She felt bad for him and his family, and suddenly understood why he had been so defensive of Shanty Row and embarrassed to bring her here.

It was proof positive that he was an undesirable—in this world.

"'Tis a sorry tale, how we ended up on the Row," Annikki said, shaking her head.

"Mama," Otar quietly interjected, standing up, "'tis no need to bore Madalyn with our life history." He leaned down and kissed her cheek. "I must go to the grindstone and work. I will see you at the evening repast."

"I'm not bored," Madalyn countered. "I'm very interested." The last part of what he had said slowly dawned on her. "You're leaving?"

"Only to work. I shall return, Madalyn."

"You needn't look aggrieved, daughter," Annikki assured her. "Naught will happen to you whilst he is away."

"I'm not distressed." She attempted a scoffing look but suspected she fell short. "Well, maybe just a little," she muttered.

Madalyn had expected to feel relief if he ever left her; instead, she felt dread and more than a little insecure. Otar was many things—her captor, her defeater, her subjugator—but he was also her protector.

Still, she didn't want to appear a weak little ninny. It was bad enough that she already looked like a raging slut. "I'll be fine," she told Otar. "Really."

Otar slowly inclined his head. "You will spend the day with my mother and sister. All will be well, Madalyn."

"I know."

He bent down and kissed her cheek. Annikki and Agata smiled, dreamy expressions on their faces, as if Otar and she were the love match of the millennium. Madalyn delicately cleared her throat and accepted the kiss.

After the door had closed behind him, she turned back to the other women. "So . . ." She smiled at Annikki. "Please go on."

"Eh?"

"You were telling her the saga of how we came to live here," Agata reminded her.

"Oh, aye." Annikki chuckled. "The old memory isn't what it used to be, I fear."

"Now," Madalyn said, steering back to the point, "you were saying . . ."

OTAR RAISED THE HAMMER high above his head and struck down hard on the metal below. He repeated the action as he sweated heavily, needing the release it provided.

Right at this very moment, Madalyn was learning about his past and his present. He had hoped his mother and sister wouldn't inform her that she'd wed the most undesirable man in all of New Sweden—at least not until he had captured his wife's love.

All would be lost now. No wench would want the black mark of being married to an outcast, of knowing that any children she might bear were marked as undesirables before they were even conceived.

Could he blame her? Nay, he could not. Were he a wench, he wouldn't wish to marry such a man as himself, either.

He shouldn't have claimed Hunter's Right, forcing Madalyn to his side for all times. Aye, he wanted her, but it wasn't fair to force her into such a humble, pitiful life in Shanty Row.

"You look like someone died."

Otar glanced up at the sound of his cousin's voice but didn't cease his exhaustive labor. "You aren't one to talk."

"Wench troubles?" Nikolas ventured.

"Aye. You?"

"Aye."

They shared a commiserating look. His breathing heavy, Otar leaned back on his hammer.

"She will never love me," Otar said, coming straight to the point. "Who could love a man on Shanty Row? 'Tis why none of the poor sods ever wed."

"'Twill not be that way always, cousin," Nikolas promised. "Leastways, I will make things better for those on Shanty Row after the Revolution." He looked at him pointedly. "And you shall be reinstated as the rightful heir to your sire's estate."

Otar didn't even know if he'd live through the Revolution. Still, if he didn't, it was a relief to know that Nikolas would see that she dwelled in the luxury of Thordsson Longhouse.

"So what are your troubles?" Otar asked. He didn't feel like talking of Madalyn right now; 'twas a sore subject. "You've a grand estate."

He grunted. "Ronda thinks our people to be barbarians. She won't even speak to me."

"She will come around," Otar reassured him.

Nikolas smiled. "Mayhap you should take your own advice."

That was different—vastly so. Otar was already preparing himself for being rebuked by Madalyn upon his return home. He couldn't blame her, yet neither could he stop mourning the loss of any love that might have blossomed.

But this was not Lord Ericsson's woe to endure. He had enough on his mind, preparing for the war that lay ahead.

"Mayhap I should," Otar said noncommittally.

Nikolas patted him on the back and left the grindstone.

MADALYN LISTENED WITH A HEAVY HEART as Annikki told her how they had all ended up on Shanty Row. Otar had lost so much, and for reasons so shallow.

"That's terrible," Madalyn said, her heart wrenching. "I can't believe that Toki character got away with it."

"Nor can I." Annikki's sigh was weary. "'Tis glad I am my husband died before Toki rose to power. 'Twould have torn his heart asunder to watch my sire's home snatched away by foul hands."

"What about Otar? I'm sure it was difficult on him, too."

"Aye, it was," Agata interjected. "He has spent his entire life preparing for battle. He is obsessed with regaining all that was lost. Not for himself, but for us."

Madalyn stilled. "He's going to a battle?"

"The Revolution," Annikki clarified, her voice lowered to a hush. "I do not want Otar to join it, yet I know he cannot be swayed." She went on to explain what the Revolution was and why it was occurring. "Death will come to many before the jarldom is reclaimed. I could not bear it, did I lose my son."

Madalyn's stomach was in knots. She supposed a captive bride shouldn't care if her husband died in battle, but she did. Much more than she wanted to admit.

Madalyn covered the older woman's hand with her own. "Otar is the strongest man I've ever met. He will make it through alive, no matter what lies ahead."

"Well," Annikki said, changing topics, "would you like to see more of Shanty Row? Agata and I would be pleased to give you the tour."

Madalyn inclined her head. "Sure. That sounds good."

Chapter Eighteen

"*There isn't much good to see here,*" Agata warned her as the trio made their way from the Thordssons' adjoined huts. "But 'tis wise to be familiar with the layout of the land."

"I'm sure there's got to be something redeemable about your village," Madalyn demurred with a sincere smile. "I'm looking forward to seeing it."

Annikki and Agata shared a glance that said they wished Madalyn was correct, but she wasn't. She swallowed, not really sure what to expect of the tour, but suddenly a bit nervous about it.

"This is where the children of Shanty Row gather and

play." Annikki gestured toward something that resembled a pig's trough with five filthy kids wrestling in it.

Madalyn smiled at the children, who, not knowing any better, laughed and giggled like the richest people on earth. They had only a tiny bit of dirt and clay to play in, but they managed to make it look fun. Kids were kids no matter where you went, and these little ones were no different. Boisterous and rowdy, they took playtime quite seriously.

"The babes of this village are few in number," Agata explained as a boy ran up and greeted her in their native tongue. She grinned at him, affectionately ruffled his hair, and sent him back to play with the other children. "So they are deemed treasures here. All those on the Row care for and love them as though they were their own children."

"That's wonderful. But why are there so few children?"

"Hardly any men can afford wives," Annikki informed Madalyn. "Only the most desperate of sires allow their daughters to enter an auction where Shanty Rowers are permitted to bid on brides."

"I see." Annikki and Agata didn't flat-out say so, but she could tell they believed life here was a wretched existence. She couldn't help agreeing. "That's terrible."

Madalyn followed the other two women down a narrow alley. "Why is it so quiet here?" She asked.

The place looked like a ghost town, and it gave her the creeps. Drake's mind would have had a field day with all these deserted alleys and shacks. Otar had been correct—if you'd seen one hut you'd seen them all. Still, most of the huts looked to be faring far worse than his. The Thordssons seemed rich in comparison.

"Most of those on the Row are men," Agata explained. "They toil in the mines for a few coins thrown their way. So they are gone working all day."

Male laughter and whistles reached Madalyn's ears, the sound at odds with Agata's previous statement.

"'Tis the alehouse of the village," Annikki responded, as if reading her mind. "The alehouse is the only establishment in Shanty Row that those of higher classes frequent. The voices you hear belong to males of the upper classes, not the men who dwell here."

"Why do they come to Shanty Row for food and drink?" Madalyn asked. She honed in on the cobblestone building that was built much more sturdily than anything else in the area. "Don't they have their own pubs?"

"Aye," Agata said acerbically, anger apparent in her voice. "Yet they cannot get as many creature comforts in those alehouses, so they choose to come here, pandering for favors like the vermin they are."

"This is where the majority of daughters and wives of Shanty Row must make their wages." Annikki sighed. "We are fortunate that Lord Ericsson pays Otar well enough to keep us from the same fate."

Madalyn had no idea what they were talking about. Approaching the cobblestone structure, she decided to keep her mouth shut and ask questions later.

"Go on," Agata whispered. "Take a look inside."

"Be careful not to be seen!" Annikki warned in a hushed voice. "You do not covet the attention of any man in that place."

Curiosity consumed Madalyn. She made her way behind a large boulder and peered up over it. Much of the building was designed like an open cantina, overhead fans and all, so eavesdropping was relatively simple. When she got a gander at what lay on the other side of the rock she was hiding behind, she had to remind herself she couldn't make a sound, not even a gasp of astonishment.

This certainly explained a lot of what Annikki and Agata had said. Her heart sank for the poverty-stricken women of the village whose lot in life was serving men of the upper classes.

Being a waitress wasn't so bad—Madalyn had done it before stardom had come knocking—but doing it naked, and while anything with a penis groped and fondled you, was beyond humiliating. She felt so sorry for the women that her heart ached.

Madalyn's disbelieving gaze honed in on one female in particular. She was strikingly beautiful with long, blond hair and clear blue eyes that could be seen all the way from her hiding place. Her body was perfect, trim where men liked for it to be and plump where they preferred. Her breasts jiggled as she walked, toting three mugs of ale over to a group of drunken, loud men. The men's conversation, once in Old Swedish, switched to English. Madalyn wondered why.

The waitress set the mugs before the three men. She didn't so much as bat an eyelash when one of those males grabbed her breasts and started sucking on her nipples. She stood there while he played with her, obviously used to such behavior.

The older, drunken male released her nipple with a popping sound. She straightened her back and demurely folded her hands behind her back. The patron held up a coin and grinned. "Show me your treasure if you want this, wench." He wiggled his eyebrows as his two friends laughed. "Spread 'em wide."

She did as requested with nary a word of protest. Hopping up onto the small table, the serving girl sat down in front of him and, palms resting on the table's edges, splayed open her legs. As his beady, aroused eyes studied her slick folds intently, he all but drooled.

"You've such a pretty pussy," the man purred as he began fondling her. He frowned. "But I thought I told you to shave it."

She gave him the chastised look he sought but didn't speak a word. She probably wasn't permitted to; she was expected to just sit there until he waved her away or was sent to another table.

"I could play with this pussy all day." The man bent his head and flicked at her clit with his tongue several times in rapid succession. "But, alas," he told her, giving her the coin, "I've business to discuss with my men." He waved her away. "Be gone until I summons you again."

Madalyn felt sick. *This* is how the women of Shanty Row helped earn wages for their families? *This* was what Annikki and Agata—and herself—would have been sentenced to had Otar not found a way to prevent it? She shivered. Madalyn would have rather been dead than subject herself to such a dehumanizing ordeal on a daily basis.

"Come," Annikki whispered, tugging at her hand. "You've seen enough."

"More than enough," she agreed, tearing her eyes away. "Can we go back home? I feel rather ill."

"'Tis sorry I am you witnessed that," Annikki said, her smile sad. "But you needed to understand the lot of life here, and how fortunate we are in comparison."

Madalyn got the picture loud and clear. Blowing out a breath, she followed Annikki and Agata back toward the Thordsson huts.

"WELL," MADALYN SAID as she plopped down at the kitchen table. "That was an eye-opener of an experience. In fact, I doubt my eyes will go back to their normal size for at least a month."

"Again, you've my apologies, daughter," Annikki said, covering her hand. "I'm beginning to lament taking you to that evil place. I should have—"

"It's all right." Madalyn dismissed her regrets. "You were correct—I did need to see it. And yes, I can also see that life in these adjoining huts is a much better one than most women have here."

Agata sighed. "Mayhap we should have prepared you better. 'Tis a sad sight."

Madalyn had seen plenty of the seedy in her days as an actress. Granted, she'd never seen something so wretchedly heartbreaking, but a couple of things had ranked close. Scummy casting directors "requesting" sexual favors prior to letting a wannabe actress try out for a part, eager fans groping anywhere they could touch . . .

But nothing compared to that awful place. The alehouse was as bad or worse than the bride auction block, which was saying a lot.

"There's got to be something we can do to stop it," Madalyn said, her mind racing. She glanced at both women. "I mean, there has to be another way women can earn wages around here other than being forced to do . . . well . . . *that.*"

Annikki harrumphed. "If you think of a way, share it with us all. I can't imagine anyone patronizing an alehouse in Shanty Row unless the wenches be naked and docile."

"'Tis true," Agata agreed. Otar tried to think of ways to help them when first we were sentenced to the Row. My brother is known for his cunning, yet not even he could think of an escape from their lots in life."

There had to be *something.* There was *always* something. It was just a matter of figuring out what it could be.

Annikki gasped. "I've an idea." She smiled slowly. "I never would have thought of it had you not come to dwell here," she told Madalyn, "but I believe 'twill work."

"You've got my attention. What is it?"

Chapter Nineteen

Otar came home from the grindstone and found the trio of women right where he'd left them hours earlier: sitting at the table, talking and eating, smiles and laughs abundant. 'Twas a pleasant sight, and one he'd never thought to have for his very own.

The Thordsson women were so engaged in their conversation that they didn't even hear him approach. He stood back in the shadows and watched, enjoying their banter.

"Do you really think we should?" Madalyn asked, her nose wrinkling.

"I think 'twould be fun!" Agata laughed, her excitement

evident. "And I also think 'tis the perfect way to earn coins on the Row."

"As do I," Annikki concurred. She patted her blond hair and affected a haughty pose. "I should like to be one of the stars of the saga. I will be the fetching widow coveted by so many warriors."

Peals of laughter ensued. Otar's eyebrows inched up as he wondered what they were talking about.

His mother patted Madalyn on the hand. "New Sweden has no theaters to speak of, and plays are a rare treat in this world. 'Twill be a wondrous distraction for our people, as well as a good way to help those on the Row. 'Tis also a fun way to pass the time."

"Especially your time, whilst you settle into the way of things here in Lokitown," Agata added.

"I doubt that will ever happen." Madalyn's smile dissolved. "I don't mean any insult, but I can't accept that I'll never lay eyes on the outside world again."

Otar's muscles tensed up. He would give anything to make her happy, but letting her go wasn't possible. Even if he wanted to set her free, no noble of the Underground would permit it.

"I can't begin to imagine how difficult this is for you," Agata said softly. "As wretched as Shanty Row is, I'd much rather be with the devil I know than the one I don't."

"Exactly!" Madalyn said, spreading her hands. "It might not be the most ideal situation, but it's still familiar to you."

Annikki clucked her tongue. "I have seen fifty and four

years and many an Outsider bride in my lifetime. Every last one is possessed of the same mind-set when first they arrive."

Otar watched Madalyn chew on her bottom lip. Gods, he wanted her to accept life here—to at least give it a fair chance.

"But I'll tell you something," Annikki continued, raising a finger. "All of those wenches are happy now, their lives bliss. The only difference between them and you, daughter, is time. They have come to terms with the will of the gods, and you have not."

Madalyn seemed to really be listening. Otar wanted to let his mother continue, for she seemed to be faring far better at changing his wife's mind than he had. But he also realized 'twas not his mother's responsibility; 'twas his own.

Another thing Otar noticed was that Madalyn didn't seem put off by his mother and sister, even though she now knew they were undesirables. Would her kindness extend to him, as well?

Clearing his throat, Otar stepped into the hut. As always, his mother and sister greeted him with smiles. Glancing toward Madalyn, he awaited her reaction. Her expression unreadable, it felt nigh unto forever before she spoke.

Her lips curved into a warm smile. "Welcome home," Madalyn said, her gaze searching his. "Did you have a good day?"

Otar was too relieved to speak. It took him a moment to recover. "Aye." He scratched his chin. "'Twas passing fair."

She nodded. "Good."

"And yours?"

"It was pleasant. Your mother and sister are wonderful."

He wanted to ask about her aspiration to perform plays in Lokitown, but if he did so they would know he'd been listening at the door. "I should bathe before the evening repast," Otar announced.

"Aye," Annikki agreed. "Agata and I shall go fetch the food and bring it over anon. Or would you two prefer to eat next door?"

Otar looked to Madalyn, his expression inquiring.

"Next door would be great," his wife answered. "I could do with a change in scenery, even if it's only a few feet away."

At Otar's nod, Annikki motioned for Madalyn to follow her. "You know where to find us, son," she said over her shoulder while heading toward the connecting door.

Madalyn stopped at the door and glanced back, her gaze finding his. She stared at him for a suspenseful moment, then blinked and walked away. Otar stood gazing after his wife long after the door shut behind her.

Chapter Twenty

"*Mayday! Mayday!* I'm calling in a one-niner-niner! Hello? I've got a one-niner-niner!"

"Uh . . . sorry, but I'm new. What's a one-niner-niner? Hang on and I'll look it up in the CACW manual."

Drake tore the mobile phone away from her ear and stared at it like it had sprouted horns. Either Big Brother had taken over CACW headquarters, or Chaz Thorton, the secret facility's director, was letting one of his dopehead friends answer the phones again.

"Nope," the disembodied voice continued over the phone line. He inhaled deeply, taking a drag off what was presumably an illegal cigarette. "I don't see nothin' about a one-niner-niner. You better explain it to me."

Drake blinked. "I've been kidnapped with my sister, forced to marry an alien—or a man with an inhuman ability to sexually intrigue hapless women—and then I escaped. Now I need help."

"Weird! Are his eyes too blue?"

She nodded grimly. "Unfortunately so."

Another inhale. "I read a story like that in the tabloids yesterday. Some chick in Arkansas gave birth to a fork-tongued half-breed. You can guess what color the baby's eyes are."

Drake whimpered. She didn't need to hear this on the heels of having thrown herself at Iiro like a possessed slut on speed.

"Listen! I don't have time to swap field stories. Right now I need help. I'm not out of danger yet and my sister is still a captive."

Silence.

"Hello?" Drake frowned. "Mayday! Hello?"

The sound of faint snoring reached her ears. Her jaw dropped. Preparing to screech into the CACW-issued mobile, she saved her breath when a telltale buzzing sound ensued.

The connection was dead. She swallowed roughly, fear lancing through her.

Baaaaaaaa. Baaaaaa. Baaaaaaaaaaa.

Drake grunted at Victoria and Thor. Uncertain of what

to do with the goats upon her arrival, she'd let them come into the log cabin with her. Spotting some apples that had been set on Madalyn's kitchen counter, she tossed them over to the duo, then began to pace.

She didn't know what to do, where to go, or who to turn to for help. She had tried to alert CACW several times since she'd made it here an hour ago, but each attempt had been met with failure. She'd thought the heavens had answered her prayers when she finally heard another voice on the line. Wrong.

Think, Drake, think! Iiro is going to come looking for you. You've got to leave this place.

But where should she run to?

There wasn't time to think. There was time to snatch the camera from its hiding place and run like the devil was chasing her. With Iiro tracking her scent, the analogy wasn't too far off base.

There was something about that damn man, some potent poison he must give off. Only a toxic amount of alien pheromone could have caused her to behave the way she did. She frowned, recalling that she'd rode him more aggressively than the Lone Ranger had galloped on Silver.

Hoisting up the floorboard, Drake snatched the camera out of its hiding place. Setting the board back in place, she stood up and barreled toward the front door.

Baaaaaa. Baaaaaaa.

Jarring herself to a stop, she looked at the goats. She

muttered under her breath, figuring the pheromone had also made her a sap.

"Let's go," she said dejectedly, sighing. "We've got a one-niner-niner."

Her eyebrows rose when Victoria and Thor baaaéd and followed. At least somebody understood CACW code.

Chapter Twenty-one

The days that followed were routine in structure but far from ordinary in practice. Madalyn spent much of her time with Annikki and Agata, practicing the play they hoped to put on in the alehouse very soon. She spent her mornings and evenings talking to Otar, getting to know him.

The nights were Otar's, too. He held her until she fell asleep or believed she'd fallen asleep. More than once Madalyn had feigned a deep slumber while he played with her nipples and softly worked her body into a fever pitch. It took all of her strength not to turn to him and beg him to finish what he'd started. Not just because he'd aroused her, but because along with that arousal, a trust and friendship were blooming.

Hurry up and rescue me, Drake. I'm falling for these people and I'm falling hard.

"'Tis your scene here, Mama," Agata told Annikki, breaking Madalyn from her reverie. "This is where Hilda admits her love for Joonas."

Madalyn grinned as Annikki took the small stage they'd erected. As she'd wanted, Otar's mother was the fetching widow coveted by so many warriors.

Annikki was a natural. Madalyn loved to watch her perform. She would have made millions above the ground with her wispy, blond good looks and dramatic presence.

"I suppose I'll have to play the part of Joonas for now," Madalyn said, walking toward Annikki. "We still have to find some male actors."

"I believe I would make the best Joonas."

The women turned at the sound of the male voice. A strong, tall, older Viking man stood by the door of the hut. A very good-looking man, he possessed an exceedingly powerful build. His gaze never strayed from Otar's mother.

"Nay, you would not," Annikki said, rolling her eyes. "Do we need the part of a dunce, I will be certain to inform you."

Madalyn's eyes widened. She'd never heard Annikki be so rude to anyone.

"Mama," Agata bit out, her voice chiding, "do not be so churlish to Vardo."

Vardo looked more amused than offended. "Ah 'tis fine, Agata. I am used to your mother's vulgar ways," he quipped back. He held a hand over his heart. "'Tis why I love her so."

Annikki frowned. "I am not vulgar. Now get the hell out of here."

Madalyn all but choked. Vardo did nothing but laugh. She got the feeling that they'd known each other a long time, and had been playing cat and mouse for just as long.

Vardo clucked his tongue. "I did not come here today to exchange barbs with you, wench. Mayhap on the morrow I will come back for that."

"Joyous news indeed," Annikki said sarcastically. "Then why are you here? Tell me so you can leave."

"To meet Otar's new bride, of course."

"How unfortunate for my daughter-within-the-law."

"Mama," Agata scolded. "Mind your tongue." She smiled up at the big man who was obviously head over heels in love with Annikki despite her attempts to thwart him. "Vardo, this is Madalyn. Madalyn, meet Vardo. Vardo is much like an uncle to my brother and me. He was our sire's best friend from childhood until his unfortunate death."

Madalyn walked over to greet him with a smile. "It's a pleasure to meet you."

"Likewise." Stopping midbow, Vardo's eyes widened as he got a good look at Madalyn's face. Grinning, he shook his head and chuckled. "I see why he wed you. You look like Victoria."

"Victoria?" Annikki said. "Otar knows naught of a Victoria. Do not attempt to compare her to another wench!"

"I did not mean insult. 'Tis sorry I am—"

"It's all right," Madalyn told them both. She sighed, then admitted, "He's not comparing me. I *am* Victoria. I mean, I'm the woman who played Victoria in the movie he's referring to."

Vardo swallowed. "You are Victoria?" He glanced down at her breasts, then back up to her face, and his grin returned. "Cheers for Otar. He always said if he knew where to find you, he'd steal you as his bride in a heartbeat." He wiggled his eyebrows. "Looks like he got his chance."

Madalyn shifted topics, not in the mood to relate how she'd really gotten here. "How long have you known Annikki?" she asked.

"Too long," Annikki muttered. "He is like an illness that refuses to go away."

"I love you, too, my beauty."

Annikki threw her hands up, exasperated. "I daresay you are the dunce I thought you to be. Leastways, you have met my daughter-within-the-law. Now be gone!"

If there was one thing to be said about Vardo, he wasn't easily offended. Or easily swayed. "Does this mean we will not be having sex this eve, my love? 'Tis fine. I prefer to wait until the eve we are wed to consummate."

"Since that occasion shall never arrive, so do I."

Bemused, Madalyn watched them exchange insults for another solid minute. Or rather, Annikki insulted Vardo and Vardo chuckled and enjoyed it. If Madalyn wasn't mistaken, the gleam in Annikki's eyes meant she relished their banter as well.

Why did they go through all of this fuss? They should just get together; it was obvious they cared for each other.

Agata said under her breath, "It usually lasts another minute or so, then he will leave and Mama will pretend she doesn't care."

"Why? I don't understand her reasoning."

Agata sighed. "She fears that Toki will have Vardo killed if she weds with him. 'Tis why she pushes him away, though he doesn't know it's her motive. The only reason I know is because I overheard her crying one morn whilst she prayed to the gods for the strength to turn her back on Vardo."

"That's so sad." Madalyn shook her head. "I feel terrible for Annikki."

"As do I. But her reasons are real, Madalyn, so do not push the subject."

"Why would Toki kill him?"

"Because a marriage between them would raise our status. We could leave Shanty Row."

Madalyn looked at her quizzically.

"Vardo is of the noble class."

UPON BEING SUMMONED, Otar entered the vast planning chamber in Lord Ericsson's dwelling. Something important had to be brewing, or Nikolas would have waited until the end of the working day before gathering the men together.

The Revolution sympathizers his cousin had sent for totaled twenty. All hailed from his private inner circle. All were trusted confidants, some of them to a greater degree than were others, but all were held in esteem.

The ranks of the men varied from lords to soldiers. Only a handful of lords were present, but there weren't many nobles left to speak of. Several of them had died in less than godly fashions after Toki claimed the throne.

Below the ranks of the nobles were the warriors, the caste Otar belonged to. It was rare for a Shanty Rower to possess such a place in life; in fact, it had never been done before. But 'twas not Toki who had decorated Otar, but Nikolas.

The warriors commanded the third caste, the soldiers, and together they were entrusted with the majority of the battling. 'Twas rare to find a noble who would fight. Nikolas and Vardo were the exceptions, but they were not weak and frightened as nobles were wont to be.

Otar's eyebrows drew together when Otrygg and his nephew Erikk entered the planning chamber in lieu of Nikolas. The men were devout loyalists of Lord Ericsson. Still, 'twas not like his cousin to fail to show up to his own meetings.

"What goes on here?" Vardo grumbled, frowning at the men. "Where is Niko?"

Otrygg held up his hands to command quiet when others began to ask questions as well. "Silence!" he bellowed, a tic working in his jaw. "We don't have much time to prepare!"

His announcement produced the desired effect. 'Twas hushed enough to hear a rat sneeze.

"Lord Ericsson treks to New Norway as we speak," Otrygg told the men. "He will barter for more weapons and return anon."

Otar's eyes widened. That voyage wasn't slated to happen for another fortnight.

"Prepare your men for war!" Otrygg cried. "We hold up our swords upon Nikolas's return from New Norway!"

Shouts of approval punctured the air. The men grinned, slapping each other on the back.

"Why now?" Otar asked. "We agreed on two fortnights from now."

"There are many reasons," Erikk answered for the elder Otrygg. "We had thought to discuss all of them this eve with the lot of you, but some disturbing news has reached our ears since Lord Ericsson set sail in the Underground waterway. We must speak of this instead."

"Get on with it, then," Otar said, not one for suspense. "What has happened?"

Otrygg's face hardened. "We've a traitor amongst us."

Silence.

"What?" Vardo shook his head. "'Tis hard to credit, Otrygg. None amongst us can stand Toki. Verily, most of New Sweden would like to see him dead."

"Apparently not everyone in New Sweden," Erikk bit out. "I do not believe the traitor stands in this chamber, but 'tis someone that we believed to be faithful to our cause."

"Whispers of the Revolution have reached Toki's ears," Otrygg said. "He readies himself for battle as we speak."

Otar's thoughts turned to Madalyn. How would he tell her he had to leave? Should he even tell her?

The past week with his wife had been the greatest of Otar's life. A deep friendship was forming, a mutual respect and trust. 'Twas more than he had expected so early in their relationship. He had hoped they would have more time together before the inevitable came to be, but time had run out.

"Two days," Otrygg announced. "You have but two days left to you before we strike."

Chapter Twenty-two

"*Hi.*" *Surprised Otar was home so early,* Madalyn stood up to greet him. She had been cutting up the apples Annikki had brought her to make tarts with this evening. "An early day?"

Otar nodded, his appearance distracted. "Madalyn, we must talk."

"Okay," she said slowly, setting down the knife. "What's going on?"

He was dressed in his usual clothes—brown animal skin braes tucked into heavy black boots that stopped just below the knee, a chain-mail tunic that showed off his impressive musculature, and ornate bangles clasped around his biceps.

And, as was usually the case after a day's work, perspiration soaked his hairline.

Until Otar, Madalyn hadn't realized that sweat could look so good on a man. Perhaps because it didn't on most men.

"There are things you must know." His expression was disconcertingly solemn. "Ordinarily a new husband would not confess to a new wife the things I must tell you now, since he wouldn't yet know that he can trust her to keep quiet. I trust you. And I must have a discussion with you."

His faith in her discretion pleased her, but his intense appearance was alarming. She motioned toward an empty chair. "Is it okay to talk here? Or do you want to go somewhere else?"

"This is fine. You needn't look so frightened. I did not mean to worry you."

"Too late. I'm worried. So tell me what's going on, already."

Otar sat in the chair next to Madalyn. "Has my mother ever mentioned the Revolution to you?"

Madalyn folded her hands on the table and looked Otar in the eyes. "Yes, she did." She hesitated for a second. "Was that okay?"

"Nay, but 'tis done. And it keeps me from having to explain what the Revolution is to you."

"I'm well aware of what it is and why it's going to happen."

"What else did she tell you?"

"That you intend to fight against Toki. And that she doesn't want you to have any part in it."

"She also knows that, regardless of her personal feelings, 'tis something I must do." His tone was too portentous for Madalyn's liking. "Every man has a fate. The Revolution has been mine since Toki claimed the jarldom."

She didn't know where he was going with this, but her belly clenched despite ignorance. "What are you trying to tell me? It isn't like you to talk in riddles. You are nothing if not blunt."

He searched her eyes. "The Revolution grows very near, Madalyn. I must leave two days hence."

Her pulse picked up. Sweet Lord, she felt like she was going to be sick. How could he force her to live down here, below the earth, and then just leave her?

"You will remain here with my mother and sister. All will be well for you, Madalyn."

"Forget about me," she breathed. "What about you?"

"I do not matter, little one," Otar said softly. "The will of the gods will befall me."

You don't matter? How can you say that?

Tears began to well up in her eyes. For the first time since they'd met, she wasn't able to shield their presence. "This sounds like good-bye," Madalyn said a bit shakily. "Like you know you're going to die and are preparing me for it."

His large, strong hand covered hers atop the table. "We must be realistic, Madalyn. I am but a warrior, not a noble. My blood will matter very little to either side in the grand scheme of it all."

She snatched her hand back and swiped at a tear that fell. "Then why fight?" she ground out, trying to understand. "Your blood might not matter to them, but it matters to Annikki and Agata."

And it matters to me.

"Madalyn," Otar said softly. "Madalyn, look at me."

It took all of her effort to meet his gaze—and to do it without crying like a baby.

"'Twill be all right. All of you will be taken care of by Lord Ericsson when at last he is crowned jarl of New Sweden. He has made his vow to me and I know he would never break it."

"Take care of us? What are you talking about?"

Madalyn felt like screaming and pounding on him with her fists. Anything to make him understand he couldn't leave.

Otar's thumb found another tear and wiped it from her cheek. "When Lord Ericsson becomes jarl, my rightful position as the Thordsson heir will be reinstated. Mayhap I will not live to see this, but as my widow, you will reap the benefits of that status.

Madalyn felt dazed. She was too numb to talk, too upset to do anything but listen.

"You will have the life you deserve, Madalyn. A large dwelling with servants, coins for the bartering stalls, and the protected status of a widow."

Otar's hand covered hers again. "As a widow, no man can force you into a marriage you don't covet. You can marry the second time for love." He forced a smile and brushed back a lock of her golden-red hair. "You deserve so much more than I am, Madalyn. I cannot regret this week we have spent together, but I do lament your unhappiness."

She opened her mouth to tell him to stay, to tell him that she didn't want to replace him—but he let go of her hand and held a finger to her lips.

"All will be well, Madalyn." Otar stood up, then bent down to kiss her cheek. "You've my word."

FLATBREAD, CHEESES, STEW, AND APPLE TARTS. Dinner was typical Annikka-style delicious—or it would have been, had Madalyn possessed any appetite.

The Thordssons might not have possessed much in the way of material goods, but they sure knew how to make do. In this small home, every meal was a feast to be savored and enjoyed. It was a time when they caught up on each other's days, shared their triumphs and defeats. They were the essence of what a family was supposed to be.

Madalyn sat quietly, her fork absently playing with her tart. She could feel Otar staring at her while Agata regaled him with a story, but Madalyn wasn't up to making eye contact yet. She needed some time alone, though she knew she wouldn't be getting any.

So much had happened this past week. So much had changed this past week.

Hearing the story of how the Thordssons had ended up

on Shanty Row had nearly torn her heart out. Otar was too good a man for something like that to happen to him, not to mention the wonderful Annikka and Agata.

Finding out that Otar was preparing to fight, and maybe die in the name of seizing New Sweden out of Toki's hands, had forced Madalyn into a jarring realization: she cared for him. She didn't want to, yet there it was.

If there was even a single thing about Otar worth hating, she would have latched onto it tightly and told herself the impending war was a good thing. She couldn't do that. His one and only sin had been in capturing her, but since that was a normal, even honored tradition amongst his people . . .

She sighed. Try as she might, she could no longer think of him as a monster.

Madalyn didn't want him to die. She didn't want him to leave her alone. She didn't want to be free to marry another man. She wanted Otar to stay.

Glancing up, she saw Otar still staring at her, just as she knew he would be. His gaze rarely strayed from her. Every time her eyes sought out his, she found him already attuned to her.

He was probably wondering why she'd grown so quiet. Her mood had sunk from cordial to outright depressed and gloomy somewhere after the stew and before the tarts.

I care what happens to you, and that scares me. I'm not used to caring about anyone except Drake. And I've known my dry cleaner longer than I've known you!

She hadn't asked for this marriage or wanted it, but he

was her husband. The stew must have contained a truth serum, for this was the first time she admitted that fact to herself.

Otar Thordsson was her husband. Her *husband*.

Her husband who was planning to leave her, so he could fight in a war and die. Her husband who didn't think he deserved her. Her husband who believed he really didn't have anything to live for. Her husband who believed she would be better off if he were dead.

Madalyn had donned many roles for money, most of them romantic leads. The stories had told different tales, but all of them had possessed one central theme: love happens when it happens.

It could take years for the feeling to develop, or a single moment in time. The love could be requited or it could be scorned. It could be forbidden or welcomed. But always it was there, shaping destinies and molding realities.

Madalyn realized that for a woman who had pretended countless times on film to fall in love, she had no clue what it really felt like. It could hit her square in the jaw and she wouldn't recognize it.

"I'm tired," she said, standing up suddenly. Annikki and Agata looked at her quizzically. Otar did nothing, just continued to stare at her, his thoughts unapparent. "I don't mean to be rude, but I need to go to bed."

Madalyn didn't wait for anyone's permission. She headed for the adjoining door and made her way into Otar's hut.

Chapter Twenty-three

Madalyn slowly awoke to the feel of strong, persistent fingers massaging her nipples and clit. With her eyes closed, she let a soft moan escape her lips.

"Mmmm," she breathed out, hazy with fatigue. All that registered was she was lying on her back . . . and her legs were spread wide open. "That feels so good."

It hadn't taken Madalyn long to nod off after leaving Annikki and Agata's hut. She had been so overwhelmed with emotions that she'd been asleep before her head hit the pillow.

The fingers massaging her nipples grew more demanding. They pulled and lightly squeezed, plucked and pinched.

They did everything right, just the way Madalyn liked it.

A thumb continued to massage her clit in tantalizing circles. Two fingers thrust up into her wet vagina, penetrating it.

"Otar," she gasped.

She had known that this moment would eventually come. Her eyes flew open.

Madalyn instantly became aware of the hard, naked man looming over her, and of the polar bear skin that had been flung to the floor. "What are you—"

"Shhh," he murmured, filling her with his two fingers. "Do not talk, little one, just enjoy the sensations."

Madalyn couldn't help but enjoy them. His hands, so callused and powerful, touched her with wicked brushes that sent sexual tension zinging throughout her entire body.

For a week, she'd been fighting off her attraction to him. She couldn't take it anymore. Her nipples stood stiff, her pussy was clutched in carnal agony, and she wanted Otar to make love to her.

"Please," she panted, spreading her legs wider and pulling him close. He was going to leave her and she wanted to give him a reason to come back alive. "I need to be with you. *Please.*"

He stared down into her face, his eyelids heavy. "I need to be with you, too," he murmured. He kissed her lips softly, gentle brushes that made her clench tighter, and then settled his body intimately between her legs. "I've been praying to the gods you would want me, Madalyn. If even for just one eve."

Otar began kissing his way down her face, down her neck, and onward to her breasts. Cupping one in each palm, he stared at them for a lingering moment, driving Madalyn insane with desire.

"Go on," she said hoarsely, her pink nipples standing straight up, begging for attention. "Suck them."

Their gazes clashed. She saw the yearning in the depths of his eyes. The intense, aroused gleam there told her without words that he'd fantasized about kissing her breasts for a long time. She swallowed heavily.

He brushed her nipples with the pads of his thumbs. She hissed, her back arching, pushing them closer toward his face.

"Please," she breathed out. Raw desire took over and she grew more demanding. *"Please."*

Otar's dark head fell to her chest. She sucked in her breath as she watched him lick her nipples, his tongue making long, firm strokes over each one. He took his time, savoring the feel of each one under his tongue, and Madalyn thought she might lose her mind before he sucked them hard.

"Please suck them," she panted.

Otar licked at them faster, first one and then the other, back and forth, again and again. The fast, hard flicks made her writhe and moan, but they still weren't enough. She needed more. A *lot* more.

"Who do you want?" Otar murmured. "Tell me, little one." His dark eyes penetrated hers, shifting up to look at her without moving his head from her breasts. He continued the flicking movements, making her whimper.

"You," Madalyn groaned.

Unsatisfied, he kept toying with her nipples but refused to suck them.

Oh God. Her body was on fire, her breathing labored, and relief loomed nowhere over the horizon. She was going to go insane.

"Otar Thordsson," she amended, hoping his name was the golden ticket. When he made no move to up the ante, sexual frustration the likes of which she'd never before experienced gnawed at her.

"Who am I?" Otar rumbled, his eyes on fire.

Madalyn blinked as realization dawned. If she wanted more, she would have to admit who he was to her. "My husband," she breathed out.

On a growl, his mouth latched around one stiff nipple. She moaned as he began greedily sucking on it, already close to coming. He kept her breasts cupped close together with his strong, callused hands, his mouth going back and forth between each one with hard, mind-numbing sucks.

"Oh God," Madalyn panted, her fingers twining through his black hair. Her thighs instinctively spread wider, her back arching like a cat's. *"Yes."*

Otar sucked her nipples long and hard, refusing to relent until he got his fill. Memories came back to her, confessions he'd made about watching the movies over and over again where she'd bared her breasts.

The animalistic way he sucked on her nipples forced her to realize that he wouldn't be letting go of them and moving on in their lovemaking until he was good and damn ready. She whimpered as she watched him, his eagerness as much a turn-on as the sensations themselves.

No man had ever wanted her like this before.

Otar sucked harder and harder, his fixation rivaling a kid with two lollipops. Madalyn was certain she would go irretrievably insane before he consummated their marriage.

Just when she thought she couldn't take anymore, her breathing so heavy she felt dizzy, Otar released one of her nipples with a popping sound. His dark head came up, his eyelids heavy with arousal.

"Your nipples taste as good as your pussy," he said thickly, grabbing his impressively endowed member at the base. He guided the head toward her wet entrance and pressed against it, letting her know how huge he was. "But now I need to know how my pussy feels."

Madalyn wet her lips, his words heightening her already significant arousal. "That's good," she breathed out, reaching around his back and stroking him there with both hands, "because I need to know how my cock feels."

His jaw tightened, beads of perspiration soaking his hairline. Her words had gotten to him, too. Good.

Strong arms came down on either side of her, gripping

her shoulders as though he'd never let go. "You are mine," he rumbled out, his expression intense. "All mine."

Otar pushed the head of his cock deeper into her entrance. Securely there, he plunged inside of her on a groan, his muscles corded with tension. Madalyn gasped as he seated himself fully, her fingernails digging into his arms.

"Otar," she moaned, writhing beneath him. *"Please."*

His face was taut with tension, his expression one of dominance and need as he impaled her with long, full strokes. "You feel so good," he said hoarsely, fingers digging into her shoulder blades. "I will fuck you all night."

Madalyn threw her hips back up at him as he took her, moaning at the exquisite sensations.

Otar rode her faster, guttural groans ripping from his throat. "Mine," he growled like a predator forcing prey into submission. *"All mine."*

Sweat-soaked skin slapped against sweat-soaked skin. The tangy scent of her arousal perfumed the hut. He mercilessly pumped in and out of her, making her beg for more.

"I'm coming," Madalyn gasped, her head lolling back. She bared her neck to him, the ultimate gesture of sexual submission. *"Now."*

He impaled her like a madman, the sound of her flesh clenching his cock reaching her ears. The coil in Madalyn's belly unraveled, violently bursting.

"Oh God!" she cried out, throwing her hips up at him at a wicked pace. *"Otar."*

Otar slammed into her, fucking her faster and deeper. His jaw clenched hotly as he rode her, the vein at his jugular bulging. Her nails dug deeper into his biceps, the sight of him about to lose his control intoxicating.

"Come in my pussy," she whispered wantonly, knowing what the words would do to him. "I want to feel your cum inside of me."

It was all he could withstand. His body tensing over hers, Otar slammed into her once, twice, three times more, then roared out his orgasm, his entire body convulsing atop hers.

Madalyn held on to him tightly, wanting him to feel as treasured as he had made her feel when she fell apart in his arms.

"*Madalyn,*" he panted, his body slick with perspiration. He fell on top of her, careful not to hurt her.

She stroked his back, his buttocks, as he lay there and recuperated, caressing every powerful muscle she could reach. Finally, after a long moment, Otar moved off of her and collapsed on the bed beside her.

They were quiet as they lay there together, both of them panting for air. Otar stared up at the ceiling, his eyes unblinking, and Madalyn wondered what he was thinking about.

The lovemaking they had shared had been beyond earth-shattering. It wasn't just that Otar was a skilled lover, but more the way he made her feel every time he touched her, every time he gazed into her eyes.

Like she mattered.

Like he loved her.

When finally their breathing calmed, Otar said softly, "You once told me that I fell in love with Victoria, and mayhap I did. He didn't look at her, but continued to stare at the ceiling. But it doesn't make what I feel for you here and now any less true."

Madalyn studied his profile. So powerful and rigid, but so gentle and caring where she was concerned.

"My life's path has been a difficult one, and I didn't wish to reduce any woman, much less you, to living under these conditions. 'Twas my intention to never marry. But then I saw you . . ."

He sighed and ran a hand over his jaw. "All these years, I possessed no hope of ever having a wife. I harbored only my dreams, those fantasies that are so secret to the heart none but the possessor knows of them."

He glanced at her, maybe to see if she cared enough to listen. Madalyn was all ears.

"The only woman in my life all these years has been you, Madalyn. Your name changed from moving picture to moving picture, yet 'twas you who kept me smiling . . . and hoping."

Tears gathered in her eyes. She could feel the pain in his voice, see it in his face. "Thank you," she said, her voice catching. "That's the loveliest thing anyone has ever said to me."

"I love you, Madalyn," Otar vowed. "I will go to my grave loving you."

"Otar—"

He held a finger to her lips. His expression was unreadable as always, but his heart was in his eyes.

"You needn't say anything, wife. When I leave for the Revolution, just know that my words are true."

Chapter Twenty-four

Unable to get enough of her wee body, Otar had mounted her twice more. He'd come so much last eve that he was drained and depleted when he rolled off of her the final time. Even then he'd held her, holding her close to him while he slept.

Otar's thoughts were distracted as he set off for the grindstone early the next morning. Everywhere he looked, every breath he took—everything reminded him of Madalyn.

Last eve had been the best of his thirty and four years. He had waited with infinite patience for his wife to accept their consummation. There were moments when he had doubted the day would ever come, but he had remained hopeful.

The day had come, and his wife had wanted him with a

passion to rival his own. Leastways, 'twas more than he could have hoped for this soon.

How ironic that fate had finally brought his beloved Madalyn to him, only to make him set off for war a day later. He wished he could spend these last few hours with her, loving her all day and night until duty forced him from her side.

It seemed ludicrous to toil one day before all hellfire would break loose in New Sweden, yet 'twas also necessary to keep up appearances. One never knew which man could be trusted, even in Nikolas's grindstone.

"I need to speak to Lord Ericsson," Luukas insisted to Otrygg.

Otar's eyebrows inched up. He'd never heard Luukas so angry. 'Twas known far and wide that Luukas was a bit crazed, but his fine hunting skills had caused Otar to overlook that and train him anyway. "Where is he?"

Otrygg frowned and fed him a lie. "Ill. He shan't be bothered today. Bring your question to him on the morrow."

"I need to speak to him now!" Luukas bit out. "I've already gone to his dwelling and he is not there. Why do you lie, old man?"

Luukas's words were pure blasphemy. One did not speak to Nikolas's overseer thusly.

Making his presence known, Otar scowled as he approached the men. "What is the problem here?"

Otrygg answered him. "Ask the brazen one what ails him. I've no notion."

Luukas's face was beet-red with fury. His actions were perplexing. "I need to speak to Lord Ericsson. *Now.*"

You need to speak with him, or you need to report back to your betters that he is still within New Sweden?

The thought struck Otar from seemingly nowhere. He recalled Otrygg's declaration that a traitor was amongst them. He didn't want to believe that the turncoat was Luukas, but it certainly made sense of a lot of things.

"Lord Ericsson was ill with fever when I left his dwelling this morn," Otar announced. "The servants like as not told you he was out so no one would bother him. 'Tis for the best. His fever might be catching."

Luukas seemed a bit too cheered by his words. "I suppose it will have to wait until the morrow, then." He flashed Otrygg a smile. "I apologize for my burst of temper." Nodding his head to both men, he walked away.

Otar and Otrygg stared after him.

"Are you thinking what I'm thinking?" Otrygg muttered.

That I am the world's greatest dunce for enveloping Luukas into my fold? "Aye." Otar frowned. "Luukas has always been a bit odd, but that outburst was revealing. We best send some soldiers to keep an eye on his comings and goings."

Otrygg patted Otar on the back. "None could predict which way any man's loyalty would fall," he told him. "Do not chastise yourself. Like as not both sides will run into their fair share of treasons before the war ends."

Otar knew his words were true. It was the only thing keeping him from taking the blow to heart. "I thank you."

He blinked, then faced the elder warrior. "I will go put on a good face and toil. You'd best have Luukas followed anon."

MADALYN HAD A DIFFICULT TIME working up the enthusiasm to practice the play with Annikki and Agata. Feigning illness, she took to her hut and plopped down on the bed. For over an hour she'd lain there, staring up at the ceiling, her emotions in chaos.

It was bad enough she was separated from her sister. Not knowing Drake's whereabouts was enough stress. Worrying over Otar was the proverbial straw on the camel's back.

Tomorrow her husband would be leaving for only God knows where to fight for his people, perhaps to the death. It wrenched her heart every time she thought about him getting injured, let alone taking his last breath.

The worst of it was, Madalyn couldn't even discuss her grief and fear with Annikki and Agata. Otar had sworn her to secrecy and she couldn't betray the trust he'd put in her. Drake would have been able to wring the truth out of her, but her mother-in-law and sister-in-law didn't know her well enough to press the hot buttons her little sister could.

So Madalyn was alone with her sorrow and worries. Tomorrow, when Otar left Shanty Row and his absence was obvious, she would be able to confide in Annikki and Agata so that they could lend their support to one another. Today, all she could do was stew in her own juices.

A small, nostalgic smile curved Madalyn's lips. Last night had been beyond wonderful. Making love to Otar had been an experience that far surpassed any previous sexual encounter. Not only had she reveled in the carnal, but Otar had said he loved her. And Madalyn, a cynic until her dying day, actually believed him.

Unfortunately, that made the impending Revolution even more difficult to bear. She had never felt so powerless and ineffective in her life. There was nothing she could do, no one she could turn to, to stop the inevitable clash.

You can at least tell him how you feel. Let Otar know that you care for him.

She couldn't believe she'd known her husband scarcely longer than a week. The events of every day since she'd been captured had been enough to pack a solid month apiece. Truth be told, she no longer knew if she wished to escape Otar, even if the chance presented itself. If he died, she'd want to leave Lokitown in a heartbeat. But if he lived . . . ?

Madalyn's teeth sank into her lower lip. She didn't have the answers to anything anymore. Nothing felt set in stone the way it once did.

It can't hurt to go and see him . . .

She didn't know her way around New Sweden, but she could probably ask Agata for directions to the grindstone.

Madalyn took a deep breath, then sat up in the bed. Otar needed to know how she felt. Guilt would consume her, otherwise.

OTAR'S TEETH GROUND TOGETHER as he wielded the heavy hammer over his head and struck down. In a few hours more he could stop toiling and go home to his wife. He prayed the eve would go by slowly, allowing him to draw out the length of time they had left to spend together.

He missed her. Terribly. They had been separated a few scant hours, yet it felt like several fortnights.

Brooding, he struck the metal with more force, grunting at every impact. 'Twas times like these he was grateful for his position in the grindstone. He could punish the metal, instead of picking a fight with a hapless passerby.

Several minutes and much exhaustion later, Otar laid down his hammer. Dripping with perspiration, he pulled off his tunic and hung it to dry on a rack, then sat down to rest. His thoughts immediately turned to his favored subject: Madalyn.

Before she had entered his life, Otar had cared very little about death. If it happened, 'twas just meant to be. After capturing his bride, things had slowly begun to change. After last eve, his mind-set had altered immensely.

For the first time, he pictured himself mayhap surviving the Revolution. Mental images of a life with Madalyn, of future babies and laughter, swamped him. He'd never thought to have those things; now he wanted them more than anything else.

Without the Revolution, Otar could never give his wife the sort of life she deserved. Because of that, he would feel less of a man. Even if one day she grew to love him with a passion that matched his own, he would still feel that way if they lived on the Row.

"Agata told me where to find you."

Otar's head snapped up. He'd been so lost in his thoughts, he hadn't heard anyone approach.

"Why are you here, Madalyn?" Otar murmured. "'Tis no place for a wench to be."

Gods, she was beautiful. The Thordsson women were permitted naught but rags to wear on Shanty Row, yet Madalyn managed to make the simple red dress shine with more elegance and sex appeal than any wench from the higher classes could ever hope to in silks and velvet. Her golden-red hair hung in ringlets down to the middle of her back, making her impossibly more inviting. Her nipples stabbed out from under the plain garment, reminding him of how much he desired to suckle them.

"I needed to see you," she said quietly, sounding a bit unsure of herself. "I have to tell you something."

One dark eyebrow slowly lifted. Shirtless and slick with sweat, he stood up and towered over her. "Aye?"

Her gaze broke away from his and she stared at the dirt floor. Otar stood there patiently, waiting for her to say her piece. After long moments passed by, he began to wonder if she would ever again speak.

"Madalyn?" he said softly. "What is it you wanted to say to me?" A bad thought suddenly struck him. "Mama? Is she all right? Agata?"

His wife waved that away. "I didn't mean to alarm you. I'm sorry. They are fine."

"Then . . . ?"

Her gaze, that green he first fell in love with in the moving pictures, lifted to meet his.

"Last night was wonderful," she said. "All of it. Everything you did . . . and everything you said," she whispered.

"I wanted you to know how I feel, Madalyn. I did not mean to cause you grief."

"You didn't." She shook her head, a soft smile curving her lips. "You did just the opposite. Thank you for last night. It was very special to me."

"You are welcome." He winked down at her. "And thank you for coming to the grindstone to tell me as much. I missed you. 'Tis good to see you."

"That's not the only reason I'm here."

She took to nibbling on her lower lip. He sometimes wondered how that lip managed to endure so much punishment from its mistress.

"What is it, Madalyn?" He reached out and brushed back a lock of golden-red hair. "Whatever is on your mind, feel free to tell me."

"It's just . . . I . . ."

"Aye?"

"I know you have to do whatever it is you feel is your duty." She kept her voice a hush, careful not to be overheard by anyone. "And I want you to know that I support you, whatever your decision."

He inclined his head. "You've my thanks, Madal—"

"But you have to promise me something."

"Aye?"

"Promise me you'll come back alive," she breathed out.
Silence.

"I care about you, Otar," Madalyn whispered. "The feeling grows and becomes more extraordinary every day. I think that—"

More elated than words could say, he grabbed his wife and firmly covered her lips with his. Her eyes round with surprise, she slowly closed them, wound her arms around his neck, and kissed him back with matching enthusiasm.

His cock immediately sprang to full alert, desperate to be inside her, though this was not the time or place.

He tore his lips away from hers. His breathing heavy, he threaded his fingers through her hair and sought out her gaze. "Go home and wait for me, Madalyn," Otar said hoarsely. "I'll be there as soon as the working day is done."

"I'll go do that," she whispered, her voice throaty with passion. "Just make sure you hurry." Her gaze flicked suggestively down to his manhood before rising to his face again. She grinned. "Victoria needs Thor."

Chapter Twenty-five

"Oh, for Pete's sake . . . would you two shut up?" Exasperated, Drake threw her hands up in front of her two-goat audience. "I'm not exactly thrilled with the accommodations, either!"

They had been walking for days and taking shelter in small, wintry caves by night. It would have been nice if they could have stopped in an indigenous camp for help and a decent bed—or decent stalls, as the case may be—but she couldn't trust that the Inuit villagers wouldn't hand her over to the enemy.

"You two stay put," Drake ordered, heading toward the mouth of the worst cave they'd slept in yet. "I'm going to try and find something resembling a meal out there."

Good grief! As if it weren't difficult enough to hunt down food for one, she had *two* baaaing goats to feed as well. Hopefully within another few days they'd be safely ensconced in a larger town that possessed phones, motels, and lots of hot grub.

Grumbling under her breath, Drake exited the tiny, cramped cave and set off. Her thoughts turned to Madalyn, wondering how she was faring, and then to Iiro, speculating whether he was still trying to catch her. It had been a week, and she'd yet to run into him or any of the other Underground Viking throwbacks.

"It's a good thing I escaped," she sniffed, reminding herself how fortunate she was to be trolling around on top of the tundra instead of beneath it. "So what if I'm cold, starving half to death, and have nobody to talk to but two goats. I'm free. This is a good thing."

Refusing to recall how invitingly crisp and warm the polar bear furs in Iiro's bed were lest she whimper aloud, Drake turned her thoughts back to the mission at hand: food.

A fuzzy cloud snagged her peripheral vision. She had been so busy feeling sorry for herself that she'd almost let something important escape her notice. "Smokestacks?" she murmured, intrigued. She picked up her pace, walking faster toward them.

From behind a hill, two billowing streams of smoke swirled up into the air. Chimneys—they had to be coming from chimneys!

Her heartbeat sped up as she began to jog, boots crunching on the snow beneath her. This was help . . . it just had to be! Yes! Yes! Yes! Yes!

Darting around the bottom of the hill, Drake came to a sudden halt. She had expected to discover a few houses; instead, she had happened upon something far more elaborate.

It looked like a science facility, but it couldn't be. There wasn't a Big Brother camp left on earth that CACW didn't know about.

Or was there?

Her secret-agent-wannabe side kicked into full gear. She approached the facility with caution, watching for security cameras. An hour's worth of patience—and picking locks— later, and she was inside the facility.

Drake blew out a breath. The hard part was over. Now it was time to snoop.

It only took a few minutes to determine that the small, two-building compound wasn't secure. *Why* was beyond her. Perhaps they figured that the remote location was all the security they needed?

How incredibly stupid of them. Information ferrets like her *lived* for shit like this, like a computer hacker finding and cracking top-secret codes.

At first, there didn't seem to be much to look at. None of the files she rummaged through contained anything particularly interesting or startling. In the last hall she checked, she changed her mind.

GENETICS LAB. AUTHORIZED PERSONNEL ONLY.

Drake's eyes widened as she entered the unoccupied room. Empty candy bar wrappers and discarded sodas in the garbage can gave it the appearance of having been recently vacated. Her gaze flicked up to a clock on the wall: 6:45 P.M. They had left for the night.

Drake practically drooled when she spotted three unopened candy bars sitting on one of the desks. Plopping down in the seat in front of it, she tore open the wrapper of the first one and gobbled it in two bites.

Her eyes rolled back into her head. *Ahhhhh, chocolate.*

Popping the second candy bar into her mouth, she chewed it while leafing through papers on the desk. The third candy bar was devoured as she booted up the lab's computer and snooped through the electronic folders on the hard drive. One file finally piqued her interest: the journal of a Dr. Erin Gallo.

March 7: Still no success. I'm beginning to think I'll never find the right DNA combination. Frustration is my middle name. If I don't produce some results soon, we won't get our next grant. The pressure is mounting.

May 11: I'm getting weary of the constant isolation—I don't know how much longer I can take it. I haven't spoken to or seen another human in over three months . . . except for Drs. Green and Hughes. They don't really count. As friends, we don't share any of the same interests. And since both of the men are married, dating is definitely out. (I'm pretty sure Larry Hughes wishes I'd change my mind about that one. Scumbag.)

Drake snorted. "Men are pigs. Stay strong, sister."

The scent of potato chips demanded a momentary pause in her reading. She visually scanned the room until she had a lock on her prey. The bag was half-eaten. Damn.

Drake hesitated, doubting the wisdom in eating something that wasn't still vacuum sealed. Ah, what the hell. She shrugged her shoulders and popped a chip into her mouth. Beggars can't be choosers.

May 22: The funding came through! And none too soon. The latest test gave me the result I was hoping for. A few more trial runs on the lab animals, and we'll be ready to test on a human subject. So close and yet so far . . .

October 19: As I sit here and breathe, I cannot believe that it's finally happened. I did it. I actually DID IT!!!! We grew the world's very first genetically altered human fetus and the results so far are beyond expectations. Not only could we choose the baby's gender, but his progress in the host womb is superior to that of most fetuses his age.

Drake stilled. Her eyes widened.

All these socially desolate years of hard work have finally paid off. Our prototype won't become available to the public at-large for another couple of decades, but I'll be alive to see it happen. Before I'm dead, there won't be a woman on planet Earth who can't choose the sex of her unborn baby . . . amongst other things.

Drake blinked. She blinked again. This was the kind of stuff you read about in sci-fi novels, not in real life.

"And here I thought chemical warfare was the world's worst nightmare." She took a deep breath and slowly exhaled. "Lady, whoever you are, you just took the cake with this one."

Drake printed out the pertinent pages of the electronic journal and stuffed them in a pocket. Rummaging through the lab for more food, she ballooned her remaining pockets full of high-calorie junk. That accomplished, she disappeared from the science facility as though she'd never been there.

HUDDLED BETWEEN VICTORIA AND THOR in yet another cold, snowy cave, Drake read the printout of Dr. Erin Gallo's electronic journal for the fiftieth time. She *still* couldn't believe someone would *want* to alter a baby's genetic growth, let alone actually do it.

Drake couldn't help but compare her finding to the prophetic beliefs of the New Swedes. She hesitated as she considered that—

No. She refused to even credit the notion; it wasn't possible.

Teeth chattering, Drake tucked away the papers and snuggled closer to Madalyn's pets, trying to absorb their heat. Tonight there was moisture in the air, making it unbearably frigid despite the polar bear fur and the goats.

Either I'm running in circles or the distance between cities is longer than I thought. Either way, I'm going to die.

There was no point in denying reality any longer. While Drake hadn't abandoned hope altogether, she had lived a survivalist lifestyle long enough to realize when the outlook was grim. Lack of food, substandard shelter, and below-zero weather conditions were a deadly combination.

She attempted to close her eyes and sleep, but the rattling of her teeth made it mission impossible.

"Well, well, well . . . look at what the lemmings dragged in. My prodigal wife."

Drake's eyes flew open at the familiar male growl, and her gaze clashed with Iiro's. "Go away," she ground out, "or I'll cut it off."

Damn it! If she hadn't been so freaking cold and hungry, she really would have been mad! All these days of running, only to end up being captured again? She was an embarrassment to survivalists everywhere.

Stepping into the cave, Iiro got his first good look at Drake. She must have appeared to be on the verge of death, for his gaze went from furious to worried in a heartbeat. "Here," he muttered, kneeling down in front of her. "Let's get you warm."

He wedged his way between the goats and wrapped himself and another polar bear fur around her. Drake whimpered, melting into his heat. "I-I'm so c-c-cold," she chattered, teeth rattling like crazy. "I d-don't think I'm g-going to m-make it."

"Shhh," Iiro gently chided her. "'Twill be all right." He hugged her tightly, letting her feel the power, safety, and warmth of his heavily muscled embrace. I will carry you home as soon as I warm you up a bit."

Drake was already starting to feel the ice melt away from her bones. She was too grateful and too exhausted to verbally spar with him. "I doubt you c-can carry me that far," she whispered.

"'Tis but a few feet away. I hunted you for miles, only to find you a stone's throw from Lokitown."

Drake's lips soured. She *had* been going in circles. If anybody at CACW ever found out about this fiasco, she'd be a laughing stock.

"I can't live down there," she told Iiro, snuggling in closer. Unless you had to lie, honesty was always the best policy—another primo bumper sticker slogan. "You're good in the sack and all, but it's too weird down there."

Drake could have sworn she saw amusement in his eyes. "Then I will keep you in the bed furs all the time. Leastways, you needn't deal with how 'weird' we are whilst I'm mounting you."

Hmph. He had a point.

Recalling the idiotic clothing that Iiro had forced her into wearing when meeting his parents, she moved onto her next gripe. "I don't like how the women down there dress. It makes me feel like a raging slut."

Iiro squeezed her. "'Tis my raging slut you are," he teased.

Drake was quiet for a moment and then said, "I want to take the goats with me. They belong to Madalyn."

"Done."

That was easy. "And I want to see my sister."

"You shall."

He was exceedingly pliant when she disappeared for a week. "Immediately?"

"Aye." Iiro sighed as he held her. "You will be seeing a lot of her in the days to come."

She listened with wide eyes as he told her of all that was transpiring below the ground. "How do you know this if you've been tracking me down all week?"

"Outsiders aren't the only ones with 'technology.'"

Drake frowned worriedly. "This sounds pretty serious. And I'm antiwarfare, you know."

"As am I, and all the other rebels." Iiro kissed the top of her forehead. "But a man must do his duty by his wife and future children."

Chapter Twenty-six

"Get thee hence, Joonas!" Annikki raised a delicate hand to her forehead and whimpered. "I cannot bear the temptation another moment. Truly . . . I cannot!"

Madalyn hadn't realized how much she missed acting. Granted, she usually didn't play the part of a person with a penis, but acting was acting. She felt like Dustin Hoffman in *Tootsie*—the ultimate dramatic challenge.

"I love you, Hilda," Madalyn insisted in a manly voice. She grabbed Annikki by the arms and shook her. "Damn you, woman!"

"Joonas!"

"Hilda!"

Oh yeah. This rocked. Exhilaration engulfed her.

"You are mine, wench!" Madalyn's jaw clenched hotly as she drew the weeping Hilda into her arms. "Forever and a day, you belong to me."

"Ah gods—Joonas!"

"This is where Hilda and Joonas are to kiss," Agata pointed out from offstage. Her black eyebrows shot up in a dramatic arch. "Surely this sight will be worth paying coins for. Shanty Row's alehouse will be the most popular in all of the Underground."

The actresses stood there for a long moment, uncertain how to proceed.

Annikki blushed. "'Twould cause a stampede, I fear. Mayhap we should find a male."

"Yeah," Madalyn sighed. "I think you're right."

"Joonas is already here, ladies. Nobody swoon, though I realize my good looks make it a difficult task."

The women's heads turned in unison. Madalyn had recognized Vardo's voice, but she wasn't prepared to see Otar standing next to him. Their gazes met, and she smiled at him.

"I would rather kiss the arse end of a polar bear," Annikki informed Vardo. She blinked several times in rapid succession, a pompous gesture of disdain. "My daughter-within-the-law's lips look more palatable."

"Gee, thanks. Comparing my mouth to a polar bear's ass sure makes my day."

Annikki grinned, then faced Vardo. "Be gone, dunce. We are serious actors here, not court jesters."

"Mama," Agata grumbled. "Be nice."

"I prefer to hoard my wife's kisses for myself. Leastways, you need a man," Otar reasonably pointed out, his eyes amused. "Vardo qualifies."

"That is debatable," his mother sniffed.

"Fear not, wench," Vardo told her, swaggering over to where she stood. "I can pull down my braes, do you not believe me."

"Well, I never!"

"Mayhap you should. 'Tis good for your sour disposition."

"Aaaaack!"

Vardo's laughter boomed throughout the hut and he elbowed a chuckling Otar in the ribs. "I think your mama likes me, eh?"

"Aye. I believe she does." He looked pointedly at his mother. "There's no other explanation for her rude behavior toward you."

Annikki gasped. "I am not rude! Take that back!"

"Then be polite to Uncle Vardo."

"My only son," Annikki said dramatically, her voice shaking as if on the verge of tears.

Madalyn figured she'd get a few good pointers out of this. Nobody, but nobody, could act like a mama who wanted her child wracked with guilt.

"I gave birth to you," Annikki reminded him, pain etched into her face. "You were big enough to rip a wench asunder, and yet I endured."

Otar sighed, and Madalyn knew his mother would win. She no doubt always did.

"Following your torturously long birth, I suckled you endlessly. You were a greedy little glutton, demanding milk day and night the gods would not grant me fast enough to suit."

Otar mumbled something incoherent.

"Did I tell you of the birthing? 'Twas two days long."

"Mama, Not today. Be nice. And show Vardo a little kindness," Agata hissed.

Annikki frowned as she stared at the man in question. It was a good minute before she said a word. Then, as if resigning herself to the will of the fates that had conspired against her, Annikki sighed like a martyr. "What do you know of acting, Viking?"

A slow smile formed on Vardo's lips. "I know I like to kiss. Joonas gets to kiss Hilda, so 'tis the part for me."

"You're hired!" Madalyn ignored Annikki's gasp and motioned for the big guy to join them. "Before we get to the kissing, though, you have to learn everything else leading up to it."

"I learn fast. Teach me, wenches."

For the next hour, Madalyn did just that as Otar watched with amusement. As luck would have it, Vardo was as much the natural thespian as Annikki was. Madalyn was really beginning to believe that the play would be the smashing success the other women were so certain of.

"I believe this is the scene with the kiss." Vardo puffed out his chest. "Do not swoon when my lips touch yours, wench."

"Is your breath that odious?" Annikki asked sweetly. She

held a shielding palm up to his chest when he bent toward her. "We will practice this scene on the morrow."

"Nay. I cannot return on the morrow."

"Why not?"

"We can put on the play after my return."

"Where are you going?"

"Not yet," Otar warned, his eyes on Vardo.

Annikki glanced back and forth between the two men. "What goes on here? I do not care for . . ." Her voice trailed off. "Oh nay," she whispered. "Otar? Tell me I am wrong."

He closed his eyes briefly. When he opened them, he locked gazes with his mother. "You know it must be so."

Agata's hand flew up to cover her own mouth. She looked as upset as Annikki. Little did the women know, Madalyn had been dealing with these same emotions since the night prior.

"Mama? 'Tis sorry I am—"

Weeping, she ran from the hut. Throwing open the connecting door, she slammed it shut behind her with such force that it threatened to fall off its hinges.

Vardo sighed and glanced at Otar, his expression guilty. "You've my apologies." When Otar made a move to go speak to his mother, the elder noble held up a hand. "Let me. There are things I need to say to your mother."

"Do not make promises you cannot keep," Otar warned.

"I always keep my promises." Vardo headed for the connecting door.

*   *   *

"WE'VE LOVED EACH OTHER A LONG TIME, ANNIKKI," Vardo said softly, walking up behind her in the hut. He placed his hands on her shoulders and gently squeezed. "Mayhap too long. Verily, did I have the coins to barter with at the time, you know as well as I that you would be *my* wife instead of Arn's widow."

Annikki closed her eyes against his words. Aye, she had loved him since she was a girl. And she had felt guilty while Arn had been alive, for the love had refused to wane.

"The fates were kind to you," she whispered, her eyes opening. "Did you take me as a bride, you would have been living on the Row all these years."

"I'd rather be here with you than in the upper echelons without you."

She yearned to turn around and embrace him; it took all of her strength of will to keep from doing so. "You do not mean that—"

"Aye, I do. Do not think to tell me of my feelings, wench."

She sighed. He gave her shoulders another tender squeeze.

"But the choice was never mine to make," Vardo reminded her. "'Twas Arn who won that auction. Mayhap Toki could throw all the Thordssons to the sewer once, but the law would not permit him to do it twice. If I wed with you, your family's status would be raised."

"And that is why Toki would have you killed," she whispered.

Vardo stilled. "Is *that* what worries you?"

"Aye. As well it should."

"Annikki . . ."

She whirled around to face him. Her nostrils flared. "For years, I have been shunning you that you might live without Toki's wrath. Now you think to make all my heartache for naught, and die in the bedamned Revolution?"

Vardo's heart was in his eyes. "Annikki, it must be done," he said quietly. "This you know."

She sighed, her gaze falling to the ground. Aye, she did know it. Too much evil had come to New Sweden since the old jarl's demise. Toki needed to be brought down. That didn't mean she had to like it, though.

"Come back to me alive with my son," she whispered, "and you'll get your kiss." Her eyes welled up with tears. "Now leave. *Please.*"

Vardo lightly wiped away her tears. "I'll be back," he promised her. "And so will Otar."

"May the gods be with you," she said shakily. She blinked the rest of her tears away and straightened her spine. "Least-ways, I will be sore angry with you if you die in battle."

Vardo grinned, dimples popping out on either cheek. Gods, how she loved those little dents. They'd made her swoon since she'd been old enough to know what swooning was.

"I shall bear that in mind, and I shan't die." Vardo winked. "Not without my kiss."

Chapter Twenty-seven

Otar plopped down onto the bed with a groan, threw his hands over his head, and closed his eyes. His mother and twin sister had barely spoken a word to him the entire dinner long; they had hardly looked at him.

His wife tried to keep a conversation going and managed to wring a few smiles out of them. Now she was next door, doing her best to soothe their worries. He prayed she succeeded. Hurting his mother and sister was not high on his list of things he'd hoped to accomplish before leaving to battle on the morrow.

Otar fought with himself to stay awake. His wife had lured him into returning home early with seductive glances and invitations of lovemaking, which he intended to spend the remainder of the eve doing.

He hoped that Madalyn returned home soon. He needed to be with her, sexually or not. Earlier in the day she had admitted that she cared for him; that was a good start.

There was a small part of Otar that didn't want his wife to care for him; 'twould make it easier on her did he die. But the selfish and far larger part of his soul greedily desired her love and devotion. He had loved her, after all, for years. Call her what you will—Victoria, Gretta, or Madalyn—he had loved her.

In life there were many uncertainties, but one thing she need never wonder about was his devotion to her.

MADALYN ENTERED THE HUT QUIETLY, fatigued from consoling Annikki and Agata. There was only so much she could do when Otar's death was a very real possibility.

The day she'd been captured, she wouldn't have cared. She would have been grateful that Otar was leaving, and used it as an opportunity to flee. Now she didn't know what she should do. The yearning to find Drake was powerful, but the desire to be here in case Otar needed her was equally so.

Her pulse picked up in tempo as she approached the bed, then stood there and stared down at her sleeping husband. His black hair was in stark contrast against the pristine white polar bear furs strewn over the bed. The plaited braids that made him look so dangerous and roguish while awake only looked sexy while asleep. No shirt. No pants. One muscular leg was slightly arched, showing a bit from under the furs. The animal skins draped over him from the navel down, shielding him from view.

He was so damn handsome. Not in a Brad Pitt pretty-boy kind of way, but in a Harley-Davidson bad boy kind of way.

Madalyn couldn't believe that someone as loyal, attractive, and strong as Otar hadn't been snatched up for marriage a long time ago. If she'd been a native of Lokitown, it wouldn't have mattered to her that he lived on Shanty Row. Men like Otar Thordsson were rare catches indeed.

And it's you he loves, Madalyn. YOU.

Her gaze gentled as she watched him sleep. Otar did love her—she knew it like she knew her own name. And he wanted her to love him back. She didn't know when or if she'd be ready to admit to that, but she'd told him that she cared deeply for him.

He wants much more than that. Can you give it to him?

Madalyn softly sighed. She just didn't know. She could feel something strong inside of her developing toward him, but after a mere ten days it was hard to name the emotions.

I need more time to figure things out, damn it. But you're leaving me tomorrow . . .

One thing was for certain: she'd never experienced these feelings for another man.

She stared down at Otar, the sight of him sleeping so peacefully tugging at her heartstrings. As forbidding, stoic, and deadly a man he was while awake, he looked as adorably approachable as a kitten while asleep. Well, maybe a lion cub, Madalyn mused. There was no mistaking Otar Thorosson as anything but dangerous.

There were a lot of good things to be said about her husband. To her way of thinking, the best quality he possessed was honesty. Try as she might, she couldn't think of a single person that had never told her a little fib or a big lie. Until Otar: he had never lied to her about anything.

She didn't know how long it would take her to stop grieving for life above the ground, but she appreciated the fact that her husband did everything within his power to make her feel cherished down here.

Madalyn couldn't stop gazing down at him. She sighed despondently as she recalled the words Otar had spoken to her last night:

As a widow, no man can force you into a marriage you don't covet. You can marry the second time for love. You deserve so much more than I am, Madalyn. I cannot regret this week we have spent together, but I do lament your unhappiness.

He didn't think he deserved her. He didn't think he was worthy of *any* woman's love.

"You're so wrong about that, Otar," she whispered. "No other man alive could make me question my desire to escape."

Sighing, Madalyn turned and walked over to a chair next to the hut's kitchen. She sat down quietly, not wanting to disturb his sleep. He had a long, treacherous road to haul effectively tomorrow and he needed his energy.

She, on the other hand, needed to think.

* * *

OTAR AWOKE IN THE MIDDLE OF THE NIGHT to a sight that made him painfully hard: his wife was naked and she was sitting astride him. His penis, once semierect, stood up straight.

Madalyn stared down into his face while her hands massaged his chest. Her large, full breasts dangled over him, close to his face. He reached up and began stroking her nipples, eliciting soft, breathy moans. He could feel her wet entrance pressing against the tip of his cock and it drove him crazed.

"Get on him," Otar said thickly, his gaze narrowing in lust. "I need to be inside my pussy."

Memories assaulted him. Mental pictures he'd had through the years of Madalyn wanting him and fervently riding him. Eyes tightly shut and hand pumping his shaft, he'd spilled his seed nigh unto a hundred times with those thoughts.

Now he didn't have to pretend.

Otar's teeth gritted as his wife pressed down onto his cock with her pussy. His hands fell from her nipples and latched onto her hips, holding her in place while she seated herself.

"'Twill be all right," he murmured when her eyes took on a wary look. "You can handle him."

Her teeth sank into her lower lip as she pressed down further, enveloping him just past the head. Beads of perspiration broke out on Otar's brow and he drank in the sight of her.

Sitting astride his far darker body, Madalyn's creamy,

ivory complexion was an arousing contrast. Golden-red ringlets cascaded down her back, and firm, pink nipples jutted off her large, full breasts.

'Twas heady to him that she was all his.

It was more than the way she looked. Otar had never seen a more provocative woman. Beauty was but skin deep; provocative went down to the bone.

"I'm almost in, little one," he rasped out. Gods, he feared coming before he was fully inside her. His muscles tensed as he coaxed her with a patience he was far from feeling. "Take him all the way in."

Her expression that of a yearning to be one with him, Madalyn sank down onto his cock with a gasp. Otar groaned, unable to keep his fingers from burrowing deeper into her hips.

She was fully impaled. Her nipples stiffened.

She began to move, slowly at first, but steadily picked up the pace. His nostrils flared as she rode him, her soft breasts jiggled over his face.

"You're so tight, Madalyn," he rasped out. "Love me faster."

"Like this?" she whispered in a throaty purr. She slammed her pussy down on his cock, harder and faster. "Do you like it?"

Otar moaned as she rode him, the pace growing faster by the second. Her breasts bounced up and down as her hips gyrated on top of him. "I love it," he ground out. The sound of her tight, sticky pussy sucking his cock in and out nearly drove him over the edge. "Fuck me harder."

She bounced up and down on top of him, moaning as she vigorously pumped his rigid shaft with her welcoming flesh. Otar released one of her hips and used his free hand to massage her clit.

"Oh God," she groaned, riding him faster, pumping him hard.

The sight of her tits so close to his face made him burn to play with them. Otar reveled in watching Madalyn come, though, so he continued to massage her clit with firmer, faster circles.

Her pussy clenched his cock, her inner muscles working him into a frenzy. *"Yes,"* she gasped, slamming down onto his erection, enveloping him inside of her over and over, again and again. Her flesh sucked in his as the scent of her arousal reached his nostrils. *"Otar!"* Madalyn rode him hard as she came. Blood rushed to her face, heating it, and to her nipples, further elongating them.

"Keep fucking me," he growled, his jaw tight. His fingers found her hips again, pinning her to him. "Milk my cock."

She rode him so violently he couldn't stop moaning had he wanted to. His mouth latching onto one of her nipples, Otar slammed his erection up into her flesh, burying himself inside of her in deep, rapid strokes.

He didn't want to come yet, but his body demanded that he do so. Releasing her nipple with a popping sound, his teeth gritted and his jaw clenched as he pounded away inside of her.

"*Madalyn!*"

Otar came on a roar, his entire body shaking, his toes curling. His breathing heavy, he continued to force her hips down hard onto his cock while she milked him of cum.

"I love you, Madalyn," he rasped, his voice deep and gravelly. "Thank you for being mine."

"Otar . . ."

He groaned as she continued riding him, slowly coming down in gait until she was too fatigued to continue. Exhausted, she collapsed on top of him, a gorgeous heap of golden-red hair spilling to cover his chest.

Otar held his wife close to him, the tempo of her pounding heart matching his. He wished in vain that the night could go on forever. Last eve had been more wondrous than he was capable of putting into words, but this eve was even more memorable.

This eve, Madalyn had come to him.

Chapter Twenty-eight

The emotional bond that had been forged between Madalyn and Otar last night was undeniable; she would carry the memories with her for a lifetime.

He loved her with a passion she never could have fathomed all those lonely years in Hollywood. It filled a void inside of her and made her feel complete. Madalyn Mae Simon had never been loved by a man before. Wanted, yes, but not loved. There was a world of difference between the two, and one she couldn't have understood until Otar had stormed into her life.

With a heavy heart, Madalyn watched her husband get dressed. His outfit was similar to the one he worked in every day, but this time he wore a black strap over his chain-mail tunic. The thick leather strap wound around his waist and snaked up over one shoulder. There were dozens of tiny little pockets in it, holding various weapons. Knives, daggers, poisons—if they could be obtained in New Sweden, her husband was armed with them.

In a few short minutes Otar would walk out and she didn't know when—or if—she'd ever see him again. Compounding her grief was worry for Drake's safety. Iiro had yet to return to the Underground, and she wanted to know that her baby sister was okay. Times were getting tough. Now, more than ever before, she needed Drake to be close.

Otar's gaze met hers from across the room, and she tried to camouflage her fear of losing him.

"'Twill be all right," Otar murmured. He walked over to the bed and sat down on it beside her. "I vow that I will come back to you, Madalyn."

"You better come back to me *alive,* Otar Thordsson. Don't you dare die on me now."

"I want to be with you forever." He bent his neck and kissed the top of her head. "Practice your play with Mama and Agata, and try to keep your mind occupied. All will be well."

They sat together a few minutes more, holding hands and leaning on each other until time ran out. With a sigh, Otar stood. He brushed a lock of her hair behind one ear and winked. "Stay out of trouble, wench."

Tears welled up in her eyes. Madalyn forced a smile. "I'd tell you the same, but . . ."

"'Twill be all right." He embraced her, his arms strong and protective. "Always remember that I love you."

Tell him you love him, Madalyn. Say the words!

Her pulse raced. She *did* love him. It had taken his imminent departure to admit what she already knew deep down inside, and it was time to tell him how she felt.

"Otar—"

The adjoining door flew open and Annikki and Agata entered their hut. Madalyn sighed.

"We've come to say good-bye, son," Annikki said, tears in her eyes. Madalyn blinked away tears of her own as she watched her husband embrace his mother. "I love you, Otar," she gasped. "Be safe and come home to us soon."

"I will," he said quietly, hugging her tightly. "I vow it."

After Annikki, it was Agata's turn. As Otar looked into his sister's eyes, it was easy to see the bond the twins shared. They had a history together.

"Be safe, you big brute," Agata halfheartedly teased.

The far-off sound of gunfire caused the women to gasp. The Revolution had begun, even earlier than they had expected it would.

"I must go!" Otar swiftly picked up a few more weapons and headed toward the door. "Something must be wrong. 'Tis not when we planned to strike."

"Did you hear the gunfire?" Vardo bellowed, crashing into the hut. "Let us be gone, Otar!"

The men left with long, determined strides. Madalyn ran to the door to watch Otar walk away, her throat locked up with emotion. Otar turned around and walked backward, maybe to catch one last glimpse of her before she was totally out of his sight.

Her heart pumping like mad, her breasts heaving up and down, she watched him smile at her from the distance between them. The look in his eyes told her everything she needed to know: he loved her. Just as he had promised, he would always love her.

When she had first been captured, Otar had told Madalyn that time changes everything. She had cried for her old life, not believing him.

I'm not so bad as that, little one. In time, you will grow to love me.

"You were right," Madalyn whispered as she watched him disappear from view. "I love you, Otar."

He was gone, not even a speck in the distance now.

She should have told her husband that she loved him. If he died without knowing her true feelings, she would never forgive herself.

Chapter Twenty-nine

Hell broke loose in New Sweden less than ten minutes after Otar left. Gunfire was everywhere, screams pierced the air, making Madalyn wonder how those above the ground couldn't hear what had burst below it. It sounded like Armageddon.

Frightened, the women huddled together. "We shouldn't fret like this," Annikki said stoutly. "Otar would not have left us here unless he knew beforehand that Shanty Row was secured."

That was true. Still, Madalyn was worried. Not so much for herself as for him. "This just sucks. I've never felt so wretched in my entire life. Considering everything I've gone through in the past eleven days, that's saying a lot!

"I understand."

"Captured. Escaped. Recaptured," she muttered. "Brought to a civilization I didn't know existed—"

"'Twill be all right," Agata interrupted, patting her hand. But Madalyn was in no mood to be soothed and coddled. She was getting herself worked up and there was no stopping her now. "The next thing I know, I'm married against my will. Then I'm forced to dress like a raging slut. As if all this wasn't enough, my damned husband makes me fall in love with him, only to leave me and possibly die in a war!" She raised a hand to her temples, a headache coming on. "And now people are shooting guns and God knows what else!"

"You love him?" Annikki asked in delight.

"That isn't the point! And I'm not finished bitching! I need a drink," she said dramatically. "A big, tall, fruity piña colada with an extra maraschino cherry. No, *two* extra maraschino cherries." It was time to pull out the big guns.

"She loves him," Agata said, smiling widely.

Madalyn rolled her eyes. "You two are saps, do you know that? The very definition of irritatingly sentimental."

Annikki smiled. "And yet you love my son."

She sighed, the fight going out of her. Her shoulders slumped, emotional exhaustion taking its toll. "Yes," she whispered. "I do."

It would be a lot easier if she didn't care, but that wasn't how the cards fell. "What on earth do we do?" She looked at Annikki and Agata. "What if he dies?"

"He will live," Annikki insisted. "Otar is strong and capable. He will not die."

"Mama is correct," Agata added. "Before you came into his life, my brother had naught to live for. Now he has every reason to survive." Her gaze gentled. "I cannot thank you enough for that precious gift."

Madalyn smiled through teary eyes. "You are making me a sap, too," she teased. "In fact—"

Baaaa. Baaaaaaa. Baaaaaa. Baaaa. Baaaaaaa. Baaaaaa.

Madalyn's ears perked up and her shoulders straightened. She recognized those baas. She could pick them out of a goat lineup anytime, anywhere. But how on earth did Victoria and Thor ever find their way to her?

"Would you two shut the hell up?" a female voice bellowed. "The gunfire around here is noisy enough without your constant baaing!"

Madalyn grinned: Drake! She shot up from her chair at the table and ran to the front door. "My sister!" she shouted over her shoulder. "It has to be!"

Throwing open the door, almost wept with relief: Drake was alive!

"He caught me, Maddie Mae," Drake said, stating the obvious as she tugged on the goats' leads. "I fought the good fight, but Drake Simon, survivalist, was defeated by Iiro Skevali, Alien Butthead."

"Don't call me Maddie Mae!" Madalyn laughed. "Now come here and hug me already!"

Drake's smile kicked up. Madalyn squealed as Drake ran

toward her. They kissed and embraced, Annikki and Agata watching and smiling from the sidelines.

"He dressed you in pink," Madalyn snorted, whirling her sister around so she could get a good look at her sheer outfit.

"We arm-wrestled and I lost," Drake explained in an irritated tone. "What's worse, I think the son of a bitch torched my khakis."

Madalyn whistled through her teeth. The old Drake never would have let a slight like that go unpunished.

"Don't worry," Drake said with a smile. "He'll pay for that one. Ohhhh, will he ever pay."

Madalyn laughed and then introduced her sister to her in-laws. Once Drake was satisfied they both qualified as humans and not aliens, she followed the women into the hut.

"I found something while I was out there," Drake said under her breath to Madalyn. "As soon as we're alone, I need to tell you about it."

That sounded very serious. "Okay. You don't have to wait, though, unless you insist. Annikki and Agata are good people. I trust them and you can, too."

"Wow." Finished reading the pages her sister had swiped from the lab, Madalyn blew out a breath. "Simply amazing."

"I do not understand why your people wish to control the gender of babes born to them." Agata's expression was confused. "All babes, male or female, are treasures to love."

"Not in our world, sweetheart." Drake's frown was grim. "Where we come from, boys are more important."

Silence. The sentence hung in the air, all of them thinking the same thing.

Madalyn nibbled on her lower lip. There was simply no way that the old Viking prophesies held any truth to them. It was just a bizarre coincidence.

Her elbows on the table, Drake plopped her chin in her hands and sighed. "It's hard to accept, but these head-under-the-hills alarmists were right."

Madalyn's eyebrows shot up. Talk about the pot calling the kettle black.

"I didn't want to admit it, but good grief." Drake shook her head, then switched subjects so fast it made Madalyn blink. "Can I have another tart, please?"

"Of course we were right," Annikki said proudly. "The gods of Valhalla are infinite in their wisdom." She held up a ceramic plate. "Have as many tarts as you desire, dearest."

"Thanks," Drake mumbled around a big bite. "These things rock."

Madalyn sighed and shook her head whimsically. Whether at CACW headquarters or in the heart of Shanty Row, Drake wasn't liable to ever change. For that she would be eternally grateful. It provided Madalyn with the requisite amount of normalcy from her previous life to feel semi-secure while carving out a new existence in Lokitown.

"I told you Big Brother would be the downfall of America," Drake said to Madalyn. "Hear ye, all doubting

Thomases worldwide: Big Brother has a name and it is Dr. Erin Gallo."

"Wouldn't that make her Big Sister?" Agata asked.

Drake thought that one over for a moment before nodding her agreement. "You couldn't *pay* me to live above the ground now. I'll take my chances with Alien Butthead, thank you just the same."

Madalyn snorted. If her sister didn't care about Iiro, she wouldn't stay with him. Drake wasn't afraid of anything.

The conversation turned, and Madalyn's thoughts strayed back to Otar. He was out there somewhere, possibly injured, with no way to let her know. She forced the chilling thought away.

Annikki and Agata believed she had given her husband a reason to live; all she could do was hope they were right.

Chapter Thirty

All-out war had engulfed the colony for two weeks, with no word as to her husband's whereabouts. The only thing Madalyn, Drake, Annikki, and Agata could do was hide in the huts. Shanty Row, as undesirable as it was to all others, had become one of Lokitown's few safe havens—at least for rebel sympathizers.

The owner of the seedy alehouse—a Toki loyalist—had been run out of the sector. Madalyn was thrilled to see the perverted opportunist ousted. Unfortunately, his eviction cost the majority of women on Shanty Row their jobs, leaving several families even worse off than they'd been.

Coins were becoming scarce for the Thordsson women, too, so food stockpiles were depleting at a rapid rate. Every time a hungry Row resident came knocking, none of the women had the heart to turn them away. Another week, maybe ten days at most, and the Thordssons wouldn't be able to feed anyone, because they wouldn't have anything to hand out.

Gathered around the table, the group of four tried to figure out a way to make some fast cash. With possessions being at minimum, there wasn't anything to barter with. That meant they needed cash currency.

"Mayhap we could sell some of our clothes and wear naught but rags," Annikki suggested.

Drake frowned. "Clothes can get worse than these ones? I think I'd rather starve to death."

"Me, too." Madalyn waved a hand around the table, indicating that everyone should assess their own garments. All four of them were clad in barely-there sheer dresses. Agata and Drake wore yellow today, Madalyn and Annikki blue. "None of us own more than three dresses apiece. I don't think we can afford to sell what little we've got."

"You've a point." Annikki sighed. "I don't think anyone would barter for garments of this quality, anyway."

"We could reopen the old alehouse," Agata said. "Mayhap 'twould bring in more coins."

"What's the alehouse?" Drake asked. She tucked a long, black tress behind an ear. "Is it that titty bar you told me about?"

"Aye."

Annikki gasped. "I will not have my daughters flitting

about naked from table to table, serving mead to any drunk-ard with a coin!" She harrumphed. "Though I already thought of doing that myself. I've no marriage, present or future, to taint—"

Madalyn's eyebrows shot up. Annikki serving mead naked? Huh.

"But Otar would throttle me did he catch word that his mama was doing *that.*"

"Ya think?" Madalyn shook her head. Annikki was quite a character. Her amused expression slowly dissolved. "But I think Agata makes a good point. We need money."

"The price of everything is exorbitant at the shopping stalls and mayhap will be until the Revolution ends." Agata threw her hands up, frustrated. "What choice is left to us? We've been left to fend for ourselves!"

That was what worried Madalyn the most. She knew in her heart that Otar wasn't the type of man who would leave his family starving. If he was still breathing, he would find a way to get funds to them for food.

"I can't believe our lives have come to this," Annikki whispered. "From respectable wenches to naked harlots in the blink of an eye."

"We live on the Row, Mama," Agata pointed out. "We are not considered respectable."

"Then semirespectable. None of us here are harlots!"

Elbow on the table, Madalyn plopped her chin in her hand and watched her mother-in-law's performance, hiding a smile.

"Where did it all go wrong?" Annikki asked, the air about her, looking at no one in particular. Her gaze was intense, her face angst-ridden. A better thespian had never been. "Verily, I never turned my back on the gods, yet they have thrust me from their bosom." She blinked, then looked to Madalyn. "Mayhap we should use that bit about the gods in one of our sagas, aye?"

"I like it," Drake said. "Simple, yet effective."

"Mama," Agata huffed, "forget the sagas. We must concentrate on how to earn coins. I, for one, think we should reopen the alehouse. I'm no happier than any of you at the thought of strange men touching me, but starving to death sounds much worse."

Madalyn nibbled on her lower lip. Survival was for the fittest, or at least the cleverest. Racking her brain, she tried to think of an acceptable alternative.

A play amidst a war was unlikely to go over very well. Then again, it might be an innocent, fun release for the New Swedes. Sort of like the Bob Hope USO tours for military men who fought above the ground.

She frowned, quickly deciding against it. Those specials had been free, not something the soldiers paid to see. When money was tight for everyone, it was unlikely their plays would draw paying crowds.

Unless there was something very titillating about them. Something that the people just *had* to see.

"I'm out of ideas," Drake announced. "I vote we just starve to death." Her eyes narrowed. "It would serve those bastard men right for dressing us like raging sluts and then leaving us without any money."

"You haven't given us any ideas yet," Madalyn pointed out, exasperated. "And I'm in no mood to die in order to make a social statement!"

Good God, this was just awful! Get naked and eat or stay clothed and starve.

"I don't see why you're so put off about stripping in front of strange men, Maddie Mae." Drake looked at her pointedly. "Every man above the ground knows what your boobies look like. Who cares if the men below the ground know it, too?"

"That was different!" Madalyn gasped, affronted. "That was art!"

"Art schmart. We're talking life or death here. I vote that you take off your clothes. All in favor say 'aye.'"

"Drake!"

"Just pretend you're on a movie set or whatever it is you do to rev yourself up for a nude scene."

"I got paid millions of dollars to do that," Madalyn gritted out. "There's an ocean of difference between twenty million dollars and a handful of coins!"

Sweet Lord above! Stripping for a handful of coins had HAS-BEEN stamped all over it with huge flashing neon letters—a fate worse than death.

"Money is money," Drake said pragmatically. "In the end, it's the only thing that pays the bills."

Madalyn harrumphed. Come to think of it, it wasn't that

much different from acting. Still, she had her standards. "Then *you* do it!" Her ego was smarting from the bristle to her pride. "How can I go from millions to a few measly coins? Tootie Taylor would just *loooove* to hear about this!"

"Tootie Taylor?" Agata asked.

"They are old movie rivals," Drake explained. "They hate each other. It's a trip to see them together."

Enough was enough. "I'm not taking off my clothes alone. I think we should leave Annikki out of this, but fair is fair for the rest of us." Madalyn narrowed her gaze at her frowning sister. "Either we're the three nude Musketeers or the three clothed skeletons." She waved a regal hand. "Take your pick."

The hut was quiet as the women chewed it over. They exchanged worried glances. Finally, it was Drake who broke the silence.

"Oh all right, damn it," Drake said. "I guess I can deal with it."

"Me, too," Agata sighed.

"But I'm not letting any men grope me." Drake held up a palm. "That's where the caboose ends on this train."

"I agree," Madalyn said, tossing around ideas in her mind. "We'll have to figure out something that all of us can live with."

IT HAD BEEN A FORTNIGHT since the Revolution had begun, a fortnight since Otar had seen his wife. The rebels were slowly but surely winning, gaining small victories daily.

An increasing number of sectors had been snatched away from Toki's regime and secured by Lord Ericsson's fighters.

War raged on day and night, never relenting; the death toll was climbing on both sides. Already two of Otar's childhood friends had been lost to him. One had been a rebel, the other a Toki loyalist he'd not spoken to in ten years and five.

Even though Arvid had turned his back on Otar many years hence, 'twas no easier to find him dead, his broken body lying in the dirt. Memories of childhood laughter had assaulted Otar, mental pictures of the two boys sneaking treats and eating them while they told each other made-up battle sagas.

War was no longer a boyhood flight of fancy; death had gripped New Sweden by her throat.

Thoughts of Madalyn kept Otar strong. He had but to conjure up her smile in his mind and it gave him the vigor to keep fighting—and surviving. Warriors and soldiers fell left and right, but Otar was determined to come out of the Revolution alive. His hand had slain more men than any fighter should ever have to. Thus far, he had prevailed. Otar intended to keep things that way.

"Something isn't right," Lord Ericsson said. Dressed in heavy chain-mail, Otar clanked along beside him into a secure hut that had been erected by the rebels. "From the first of the battles, Toki has been able to anticipate our every move."

"So I've noticed." Taking a seat in a chair his cousin motioned to, Otar gladly accepted a mug of ale from Otrygg, who was already in the hut. "I thought with Luukas imprisoned that the ferret had been thwarted." He frowned grimly. "I was wrong."

"As was I." Nikolas's teeth gritted. "The traitor has to be found, Otar. This bedamned war will never end until Toki is dead."

Lord Ericsson had fought as rigorously as Otar had this past fortnight; Nikolas's face was covered in the same dirt and blood as his own. He had done all he could to capture Toki, but with someone leaking information as to his every plan, 'twas an exercise in futility. Until Toki ceased to exist, his loyalists would hang on tightly.

Otrygg patted Nikolas on the back. "We will find him, Niko. Eventually all things done in the dark come to the light."

Otar snorted, amused. "You sound like one of the ancient oracles. Mayhap you can predict how many babes Madalyn will birth me?"

"Five." Otrygg winked. "If my visions serve me well."

The men shared a laugh, but Otar's thoughts were distracted. He wanted to get started on those babies anon, but first the ferret had to be found.

"Any word from your family as to how they fare?" Nikolas tore off a piece of flatbread and gobbled it up. "I've heard naught from Ronda. 'Tis driving me daft with worry."

"Nay." Otar shook his head. "I'm waiting on a report I've yet to receive. At least I know they are being cared for. I've had coins sent home every week to keep them fed and clothed."

"You'll have a lot more coins to barter with when the Revolution ends." Otrygg harrumphed. "'Twill be my pleasure to see that sadistic Nothrum ousted from your family's dwelling and your home placed back in its rightful hands."

Before Madalyn, such had been Otar's obsession. Now he just wanted to be able to protect and care for his family, regardless of where they dwelled.

Otar stood up. "I am going to get a few hours of sleep. But before I go, there is something that needs to be said."

Nikolas crooked an eyebrow. "Aye?"

"The traitor isn't a soldier nor is he a warrior."

"Go on," Nikolas said softly.

"A soldier does a warrior's bidding and a warrior does naught but impart orders from the nobles. None from my ranks know the details your ferret knew."

"So you believe him to be a noble?"

"Aye, I do."

Otar's face was hard, impassive. "I ask that you free Luukas."

Nikolas inclined his head. "He'll be free by morn. You've my word."

"Excellent. We can use another good fighter."

"Nevertheless," Otrygg said, "'twould be wise to keep an eye on him."

"I shall," Otar promised. "Hopefully there is still a trust there between us. Mayhap he knows something, but doesn't know that he knows it."

Lord Ericsson's forehead wrinkled.

"There's something strange about the way everything has happened." Otar yawned hugely. "I will sort things out after a few good hours of slumber."

Nikolas stood up and patted him affectionately on the back. "Get some rest, cousin. We can talk strategy in the morn."

Chapter Thirty-one

"*This is your great plan?*" Drake complained.

"I don't hear you coming up with a better idea," Madalyn pointed out.

"I'm not mud-wrestling you naked," Drake ground out. "No way."

"Daughters," Annikki chastised as the four women neared the closed-down alehouse, "let us not be at each other's throats. There is war enough in New Sweden without battling one another."

"That's another great line, Anni," Drake praised. "That should go in one of your sagas, too."

"I was thinking the same thing, dearest." Annikki smiled

animatedly. "Mayhap I should carry parchment and ink everywhere I go that I might make notes of my words for future reference."

"The hallmark of a great writer."

"Well, here we are." Madalyn sighed as their group stopped in front of the alehouse. "If we aren't going to wrestle in the mud, then we have to figure something else out. Let's have a look around and hope that inspiration strikes."

"This place inspires me to want to wear a gas mask," Drake said as they entered the open area of the cantina. "The tables are gross: they look sticky. Good grief, I hope nobody blew their wads on them."

"What does it mean, to blow a wad?" Agata asked.

Madalyn frowned at Drake. "It means they blew their noses," she bit out, daring Drake to gainsay her.

"*Aacck,*" Annikki spat. "'Tis disgusting. But I'm sure the wenches of Shanty Row shall pitch in and help us clean the place up."

Madalyn sighed as she gave the outside area a thorough look. "I hope they'll pitch in by doing it all." Sweet Lord above, she didn't even want to contemplate what was on those tables! "I mean, if we're doing the nude bits maybe they can do the cleaning bits."

"We can't do anything here with clothes on, let alone naked," Drake insisted. "Not until it's been disinfected."

Mr. Clean could detonate a bomb in the alehouse and Madalyn doubted she'd feel any better. The tavern was grosser than gross.

After inspecting the outside cantina, they made their way into its inner chamber. In comparison to the outside, the room was big and surprisingly sanitary. Then again, the underside of a toilet seat in a gas station washroom looked cleaner than the outer cantina.

"'Tis a rather big stage," Annikki breathed out. Madalyn smiled at the excitement in her voice. "I cannot wait to put on our saga! As soon as the Revolution ends, 'tis fame and fortune for us all."

The women shared a much-needed giggle.

After a few minutes of laughing and joking, Madalyn felt it was time to steer the conversation back to the subject at hand. "Has anyone had an idea yet?"

"Nay," Agata sighed. "'Tis sorry I am, but nay."

"Me, either." Drake glanced up at the stage and frowned. "I don't want any men touching me, I don't want any women touching me, and I don't like people in general. I'm thinking this doesn't leave us many alternatives."

"I agree about the touching," Madalyn said. "I think that only leaves us with just one alternative."

"Starvation?" Agata asked, her expression horrified.

"Sagas?" Annikki chimed in, her face hopeful.

"Suicide?" Drake inquired, clearly pondering.

"Stripping!" Madalyn was tired of having to state the obvious. *Sheesh!* "We put on one show, nobody touches us, we collect our coins, and voilà . . . food."

Silence ensued alongside a lot of dumbfounded expressions. Madalyn went on to explain what she meant by stripping. Not the raunchy, seedy, gyrate-in-your-lap shows put on in modern America, but the old-fashioned, sensual, peek-a-boo burlesque shows.

"I like the other S's a lot better," Drake said grimly. "Besides, it's not like we've got anything to strip out of. In case you haven't noticed, we're hardly wearing anything as it is."

"So we'll have to make outfits!" Madalyn held a palm to her forehead; she was getting another headache. "You're all complaints and no ideas, Drake. Put up or shut up."

"I can piece together some lovely garments," Annikki said, beaming.

"I can get the wenches of the Row together to clean," Agata added. "Mama and I can also spread the word of the show around the colony. We must decide on the date first, though."

"I can make us some homemade assault rifles." Drake nodded. "Preparation for any eventuality is the key to the CACW lifestyle."

"We're really going to do this, then?" Madalyn asked hopefully.

"Why not?" Drake said. "Besides, it might piss of Iiro, which I'm thinking is a good thing."

"Why is that a good thing?" Agata asked.

"Because he's a man and all men are pigs. But mostly because he torched my khakis."

Madalyn's thoughts strayed to Otar as the women chatted. Unlike her sister, she had no desire to make her husband angry. She was a martyr. A naked martyr. A naked martyr who prayed Otar never found out about this. And, really, he should be grateful he's married to someone so resourceful.

Come home to me and I won't have to do this at all . . .

If he died, Madalyn thought dourly, she just might kill him.

"I'M THANKFUL YOU GOT ME FREED from confinement," Luukas said. "Though I'm angered that Lord Ericsson ever thought me to be a traitor. I've been a loyal follower to the cause since I first found out there were rebels amongst us."

Leading Luukas out of the one-man cell, Otar motioned for him to follow him up the carthen pathway. "Aye, you have. And yet your behavior the other day was odd to me. I have trusted you for many years," he said honestly, "yet even I was doubting you then."

Luukas's face flushed. "I cannot help the way that I am." His nostrils flared as he glanced away. "I am not right in the head and I know it," he said quietly, "but this does not make me treasonous."

"True." Otar quirked an eyebrow. "But let me ask you this . . ."

"Aye?"

Coming to a halt, Otar turned and faced his longtime friend. "What were you wanting to ask Nikolas that day?"

He shrugged. "I was to deliver some information to him, actually. Otrygg's nephew bade me to go. He said to speak to none but Lord Ericsson."

"Erikk?" That made no sense. As Otrygg's nephew, Erikk had constant access to Nikolas. If he had something to say to him, he could say it himself. And Erikk had known that Niko had already departed Lokitown when Luukas went to hunt him. "What did Erikk desire for you to tell him?"

"All Erikk said was to ask Lord Ericsson if he could meet with him on the morrow near to the Underground water docks. I was to report back my answer, which of course I never received."

Otar's mind raced. Sweet Odin, could Otrygg's own nephew be the ferret? Erikk had as much access to information as any of the lords did.

And casting suspicion on a man like Luukas would be easy for Erikk. Because of Otrygg, no one had ever doubted Erikk's loyalty to the rebels.

"I see what you're thinking." Luukas scratched his jaw. "I say I get a decent meal in my belly and then I go hunting."

"Aye." Otar looked at Luukas pointedly. "Do you find him, bring him back alive. Lord Ericsson must make the final decision as to his fate."

Chapter Thirty-two

Another week passed by and still there was no word as to Otar's well-being. Every hour that ticked by made Madalyn impossibly sadder. She had no idea whether he was dead or alive. All she knew was that she missed him terribly and wanted him to come home.

The coins were gone—all of them. The women had spent what little money they'd had left purchasing the necessary items to make mead and food that they could sell at their burlesque strip show for quadruple the cost. Madalyn had been hoping Otar would come home before the show was scheduled to debut, but he hadn't.

Growing up in Alabama, her family hadn't possessed

much in the way of material goods. Madalyn had thought she understood what poverty was but realized she didn't have a clue until this past week. Facing starvation was a real eye-opener. It made her wish she'd done more to help those in need when she lived above the ground.

"The alehouse is cleaned, the costumes are prepared, and the buzz in the colony is that every pervert and his brother are planning to turn out tonight. We'll have a packed audience." Drake breezed into the hut. "Who'd have thought anybody would pay money to see my tits? Dumb schmucks."

"Sweet Odin," Agata breathed out as she walked into the hut with her mother. "There are crowds already forming outside the alehouse!" Her eyes were rounder than two moons. "The show does not begin for nigh unto five hours."

"We rock," Drake said. "Tonight, ladies, we become famous in New Sweden."

Madalyn snorted at that. "More like infamous." Inside, she was giddy with excitement. This felt just like the old days, with fans lining up to meet her. She tried not to dwell on the fact that the men standing outside the alehouse were just horny and wanted to see her boobs. A performance was a performance; she tried not to think on the rest.

"'Tis disgusting," Annikki muttered. "Leastways, Drake was correct—men are pigs."

Drake high-fived Otar's mother. "Don't worry. We'll dance for a few minutes, collect our coins, and send those oinkers on their merry way."

"What if men we know put in an appearance at the show?" Agata asked, still wide-eyed. "I would like as not faint did my brother or Uncle Vardo see me prancing about naked."

"There's no chance of that," Madalyn reassured her. Though if Otar showed up to see a bunch of women tantalizingly take off their clothes, but couldn't be bothered to send home word that he was all right, there would be problems, all right. Big, fit-throwing, burning-bed, be-afraid-to-fall-asleep problems.

Annikki harrumphed. "Never fear, daughter. They would like as not faint, too."

Agata looked ready to vomit. Her face, ashen, was growing impossibly paler.

"I don't think you're helping matters any," Madalyn told Annikki. "Remind me to never ask you for help with pre-stage jitters. Agata," she said, patting her gently on the back, "You will be all right. This is a one-time deal and we'll never do it again. Who cares that anyone thinks?"

It took a minute, but finally Agata started to calm down. "Mayhap you are right." Agata sighed. "I just want to do this and be done with it."

Madalyn flashed her a grin. "Just look at the bright side. You'll be one of the most coveted women in New Sweden in a few hours."

Agata whimpered. "I will be the talk of the colony, but for the wrong reasons."

"Nah." Drake patted her on the back. "Other women

will hate you and want you dead, but every man will want you. Tell her how it is, Maddie Mae."

"Nobody will think that! Look," Madalyn huffed, "we are touting this show as sort of a burlesque USO. We're just a bunch of rebel patriots who happen to take off our clothes in an effort to support our troops." Weirder things had happened—maybe.

"If they buy that, then we deserve their money." Drake grinned.

"Madalyn is correct." Annikki nodded definitively. "'Tis the emblem of Lord Ericsson that will be covering all of your woman parts. Very patriotic indeed."

"Emblem?" Madalyn's nose wrinkled.

"Yep," Drake explained, "His emblem is the dragon. Annikki made us little dragon pasties. Ingenious, huh?"

Actually, it was. It would help pull off the patriotic flavor of the show and perhaps let them salvage some respectability. Madalyn didn't care about herself, and Drake didn't give a hang what anybody thought about her, either.

Agata, on the other hand, cared deeply. She'd lived in Lokitown all of her life, and she aspired to marriage one day.

"Let's practice our dances and forget the rest," Madalyn said. "In another few hours this will be done and over with—and we can get on with life."

"Who knows," Drake said, "we might become such wanted women that they pay us big bucks to perform again."

Agata smiled. "'Twould be heady."

"'Twould not happen," Annikki chided. "Leastways, it depends on just how many coins we are discussing here."

Madalyn grinned. "So even Annikki has her price, huh?"

"Of course, dearest."

"ERIKK?" Otrygg's face was mottled red with fury. "How dare you! My nephew has too much to lose, does Toki retain his power!"

He approached Otar threateningly, as if wanting to fight. 'Twas ridiculous, for Otar was in his physical prime, while Otrygg was advancing in years.

Nikolas stepped between them. "Enough! Otrygg, you will listen to what was found out. 'Tis significant, whether you like it or not!"

Otrygg's nostrils were flaring, his every muscle tensed, but he backed off. Truly, Otar respected the elder warrior immensely and disliked causing him grief.

For a week, Luukas and Otar had kept tabs on Erikk's comings and goings. All signs pointed to a relationship with Toki. Doubting himself, even after seeing Toki's friend Nothrum pat Erikk affectionately on the back, Luukas had brought his findings to Nikolas three days ago. Niko had handled things from there.

"Neither I nor Otar took our suspicions lightly," Lord Ericsson said. "Out of respect for you, I set up a test for Erikk."

Otrygg closed his eyes and sighed. He looked at Nikolas. "And?"

"He failed," Nikolas murmured. "'Tis sorry I am."

"Your nephew was fed false information on where Niko would be at a given time," Otar said. "Not once, but twice. On both occasions, Toki's soldiers showed up for a hopeful assassination."

"Gods." Otrygg looked nigh close to weeping. "I do not understand. How? Why? What could he possibly have to gain?"

"Toki promised him a lordship," Nikolas informed him. "We are certain of that fact."

It took Otrygg a long moment to absorb it. With Erikk's sire dead, the elder warrior had cared for him as though he were his own son.

"Where is he now?" Otrygg quietly asked.

Nikolas said, "We've acquired information which suggests that he plans to show up at Shanty Row this eve."

"Shanty Row? Why would he go there? He knows Otar is at war."

"We don't know. But you can believe we will find out."

Otrygg dropped into a nearby chair. "I feel ill," he muttered.

"I will apprehend him," Otar promised. "I would not ask you to do that."

"I will go with the deuce of you," Otrygg said firmly. "'Tis my nephew and thereby my shame."

"Nobody blames you," Otar said softly. "You said yourself there was no way to know beforehand which way a man's loyalty would fall."

"That was before I found out 'twas Erikk," he seethed. "This time, 'tis personal."

Chapter Thirty-three

"*Goodness, gracious, great balls of fire!* Check out that crowd, Maddie Mae!"

Drake looked giddy. Madalyn's giddiness had long since faded. There was a world of difference between baring her breasts in a closed studio with a few cameramen and a director present, and putting them on prominent display live and in front of a bunch of horny men. In a word:

Yuck.

Sneaking a peek on the other side of the curtain, Madalyn swallowed hard. There were at least two hundred men packed into an area supposed to hold half as many. Every single table was filled, with more men crowding around those fortunate enough to obtain a seat.

Madalyn took a deep breath and slowly exhaled. She hoped their show was worth it. Nothing raunchy was going to happen, so she prayed nobody demanded their money back.

Clothed waitresses were serving mead and foodstuffs, with coins being dispersed left and right. Yes! This was just what they had hoped for—enough cash to take care of every woman on the Row throughout the Revolution. At the rate items were being sold, it looked like their plan just might work.

The show was scheduled to start in five minutes, and from the boisterous male chatter, it was clear they were ready and waiting.

"How do I look?" Agata asked, her voice breathless. "Passing fair?"

Madalyn smiled. "Way better than passing fair. You look gorgeous!"

All of them looked great. Annikki had managed to scavenge some velvety cloth and created sexy dresses. The bodices brought to mind Elvira costumes, with cleavage hoisted up and placed in prominent view, and long, slinky slits that traveled from each ankle to each thigh. Madalyn wore a black dress, Drake a green one, and Agata was in burgundy.

Beneath the dresses were leather bras and G-strings Annikki had crafted from a pair of Otar's braes. The bras were scandalous, the G-strings even worse. All three G-strings were held together by a dragon emblem at the mons.

Hair and makeup had taken a long time. There were no hair-styling products in Lokitown, so they'd spent hours teasing their tresses into sexy dos. Makeup hadn't taken long to apply, but a few days' time to make.

They were ready. Scared shitless, but ready.

Madalyn turned to her mother-in-law and took a calming breath. "The announcer's up first. Just remember to work the crowd."

Annikki nodded. "'Twill be good practice for the stage." She patted her sexily disheveled hair and straightened her spine in a haughty manner. "The audience awaits me."

Madalyn grinned. "Go get 'em."

THUS FAR, Erikk had neglected to make an appearance. But leastways, the men now understood why Otrygg's nephew planned to spend his eve in Shanty Row—'twas to watch a group of wenches take off their clothes.

The only wench Otar had a desire to see naked was the one he missed sorely—his wife. He was happy that duty required him to venture to the Row this eve, for he would surprise Madalyn with a visit after Erikk was apprehended.

Four of them sat together at a tiny alehouse table. Iiro was seated to Otar's left and Nikolas and Otrygg to his right.

"Do you see him yet?" Iiro murmured.

"Nay, not yet." Otar glanced over at Lord Ericsson, who

was dressed in a hooded cowl that made it impossible for anyone to know 'twas him. "I've soldiers stationed everywhere. He *will* be apprehended."

"Good," Nikolas said. "Then mayhap this war can finally end."

Otar was ready to respond when the lights in the alehouse dimmed. Most structures in New Sweden did not possess glowing bulbs of light. They were typically found only in large areas of assembly or on warships that trolled the Underground waterways. The majority of dwellings contained oil-based lanterns powered by whale blubber. Only the wealthiest men could afford the glowing bulbs in private dwellings.

A blue spotlight shone on the stage and the male crowd began to cheer. Otar's gaze narrowed as he visually scanned the alehouse for Erikk. A second later, a female voice echoed from the stage, the structure of the cantina providing ample acoustics for her booming voice.

"Greetings, our rebel countrymen!"

The crowd went crazed, cheering and hollering.

Otar's head jerked around, eyes honed in on the stage. He nigh unto swallowed his tongue when he saw his beloved mother.

"Holy gods," Iiro muttered. "That is Annikki, aye?"

He sounded as dumbstruck as Otar felt. It took him a long moment to respond. "Aye."

"Welcome to Shanty Row!" Annikki shouted, a full smile on her lips. Otar feared he might expel his last meal did his mother begin removing her clothing. Some things a son was not meant to see. "Sit back, order a mead and some of our fine, home-cooked food, and enjoy the show." She batted her eyelashes. "We've three gorgeous rebel wenches who will exhibit their patriotism for your viewing pleasure."

The crowd went wild as the blue light slowly faded to black. Throbbing music began to play, an old Viking battle song that had been geared up to fit the eve's theme.

The blue light slowly waxed, dim yet bright enough to reveal who was on the stage. Otar choked on his mead when he recognized the three wenches who were going to remove their clothes.

Madalyn stood in the middle, Agata and Drake to either side of her. Otar's nostrils flared as whistles and catcalls erupted, and jealousy the likes of which he'd never before experienced swamped him.

"I'm going to kill her," Iiro ground out, his gaze fixed on his recalcitrant wife. He threw his hands up. "'Tis over the khakis, you can best believe!"

Otar's expression was grim as he watched his wife, sister, and sister-within-the-law begin to dance, their arses swaying back and forth seductively. Madalyn gyrated her hips in the fashion she used in bed, slow, tantalizing circles no man but he should ever see. The audience was enthralled, dead silent as lust consumed them.

"'Tis Victoria," Lord Ericsson said, shocked. "I did not realize she'd been captured."

"'Tis my wife," Otar ground out. "I hadn't planned for

you to make her acquaintance in quite this manner, milord."

Nikolas chuckled. "Will you stop her?"

"Nay." He couldn't. Not without drawing attention to himself—the very last thing he wanted to do with Erikk lurking about in the shadows. "But believe me, she will receive a tongue thrashing and mayhap more when this show is over."

The dancing continued, all three wenches jiggling their breasts in wanton manners as they slipped out of their dresses and revealed . . .

Leather straps for clothes that induced the crowd to shout and go crazed yet again. Verily, Otar had never seen men so worked up into fits of lust in all of his life. 'Twas not the lack of clothes so much as the teasing way they shimmered out of them that was causing the ruckus.

"I must throttle her anon," Iiro ground out, his voice sounding like a predatory animal. "My hands fair itch to do it. What is that farce that she wears beneath her dress?"

Otar didn't know, nor did he care. He was too busy thinking of ways to make his wife pay for her own scandalous outfit. 'Twas made of leather—what little there was of it—and a dragon clasp was all that covered her mons. Unable to bear looking upon Agata, he concentrated his full attention on Madalyn.

Possessiveness knotted his gut. He couldn't stand to hear the whistles and cheers. Otar's jaw clenched as he was forced to sit still and watch, when he wanted nothing more than to run up on stage, throw his wife over his shoulder, carry her home, and spank her plump little arse.

"When Erikk is captured," Nikolas said, seeing Otar's fury, "I give you leave to be gone for a day."

"I thank you, milord."

Madalyn had better pray that she had a damned good explanation.

MADALYN HAD NEVER BEEN SO LIVID in her entire life. She had spotted Otar almost the second she'd ascended the stage. Relief that he was alive was quickly displaced by fury. He could pay to see a bunch of women he thought he didn't know strip out of their clothes, but he couldn't send coins back home to prevent this night from happening in the first place?

Oh yeah. Burning bed, big time.

Furious, hurt, and feeling a thousand other emotions, Madalyn wiggled out of her bustier bra and flung it to a soldier seated near the stage. The crowd went wild, hooting and hollering, several men throwing coins up on the stage.

She hoped like hell Otar was mad. That would make for an excellent knock-out, drag-out fight later on.

THE SON OF A BITCH OINKER WAS HERE. Drake briefly considered leaping over several tables to cold-cock him, but decided that pissing him off was far better punishment.

Taking things a step further than her sister had, Drake not only took off her bustier, she also sauntered off the stage to a roaring crowd, picked a nearby soldier, and wrapped her discarded bra around his neck. She jiggled her breasts in front of him, a big smile pasted on her lips.

Coins flew on stage; cheers of approval erupted. Oh yeah—the Alien Butthead was majorly pissed. *Good.*

Agata had never been so nervous in all of her life. 'Twas enough to make a wench swoon when hundreds of men cheered as she took her clothes off.

Her eyes scanned the crowd as she seductively removed her bustier. She had to do a double-take, not believing she saw him.

Lord Aleksi Pontus . . . here?

Her pulse picked up, her heart pounding in her chest. She had loved him since she was but a child, a wee girl who dared to dream that the dashingly handsome noble would bid for her on the auction block and take her as his bride.

But after Toki forced the Thordssons into Shanty Row, Agata never laid eyes on Aleksi again. For years she had prayed he would be interested enough to seek her out, if only to see how she fared. He never had. He had probably been wed for years by now.

The devil inside Agata demanded that she show the noble what he'd missed out on. Mayhap he didn't think her good enough for him, and she reveled in him witnessing so many males hoot and holler their appreciation of her form.

Agata went further than either Madalyn or Drake had. Her bustier off, her nipples stiff for any man to view, she slowly put her hands on the dragon. Teasing the crowd as she massaged Lord Ericsson's emblem, she unhooked it from the G-string, holding it in place as the rest of the bottom piece fell to the ground.

The crowd burst into cheers. She could feel Aleksi's gaze boring into her.

Mayhap he would never want her for a wife, yet Agata took great pleasure in knowing that, at least in this moment, he coveted her.

AT LONG LAST, Erikk made his bedamned appearance. Why he couldn't have done so earlier, *before* the wenches of Otar's family had proceeded to take off their clothes, made Otar all the angrier.

Leaping toward Erikk with a growl, it took Otar but one hard punch to knock Otrygg's nephew onto his backside. Otrygg was there in a heartbeat, picking Erikk up by the scruff of the neck and blasting his ears with foul words.

A handful of Toki's soldiers attempted to interfere, but Lord Ericsson had been prepared for that eventuality. Within seconds, all hell broke loose in the alehouse.

From the corner of his eye Otar saw Madalyn quickly fetch the coins that had been tossed on stage. That accomplished, the three women ran back behind the curtain.

They were safe—good. It meant his wife would be physically up to the arse spanking she'd receive soon.

Chapter Thirty-four

After tallying up their considerable booty, Drake, Agata, and Annikki had wisely decided to go to the adjoining hut. Otar and Madalyn would be having some heated words, and they all knew it.

Pacing in her bustier and G-string, Madalyn waited for her husband to arrive. She could hardly wait for him to get here; she needed to get a lot of anger off her chest. Though truth be told, she was mostly hurt.

The door to the hut slammed open. Otar stood there, a fresh cut on his face but otherwise unscathed. Only the black leather strap slashed across his chest where he kept his weapons. His hair had grown a little, falling past his shoulders. The two plaited braids remained, securing his black hair away from his dark eyes. His breathing was heavy, his eyes narrowed in anger. Every muscle in his body was corded with barely controlled fury.

They locked angry gazes.

"How could you!" they shouted simultaneously.

"Me?" Otar bellowed. He waved an enraged hand. "I've done naught but fight to protect New Sweden, and thereby my wife and family. But I see my wife was busy doing other things whilst I faced death on a daily basis!" His face twisted in pure, unadulterated fury. "Have you fucked anyone? Tell me! Tell me his name so I can kill him with mine own hands!"

"No!" she gasped. "And don't you *dare* turn this around on me!" *Typical male behavior,* Madalyn seethed. She had thought Otar was so different from other men. "You can find the time to go to a strip show," she screeched, "but you can't find the time to let us know you're alive?"

He stared down at her, his face incensed. Madalyn stared up at him, just as irate.

"I've sent home missives at least twice a sennight," Otar gritted out. "Do not lie to me!"

"You're the liar! We haven't heard a damn thing. We were afraid you were dead!"

Otar blinked. Some of his anger seemed to wane, surprising Madalyn. She had thought he was trying to turn the tables on her. Maybe he wasn't. Maybe he believed everything he was saying was true. The thought caused some of her own heat to fade a bit.

"Why did you take your clothes off?" he rasped. His jaw tightened. "It nigh unto killed me."

Madalyn met his hurt gaze directly. "We were on the verge of starving, Otar. We had no food to eat."

His eyes searched hers. "I sent home coins every sennight."

"We never got them." She shook her head. "Go next door and ask your mother, if you don't believe me. For the last week, we've been living on one meal a day."

She wanted to make the pain in his eyes go away, but first she needed an answer.

"Why did you do it?" Madalyn whispered. "Why did you go there to see women you presumably didn't know take off their clothes, when you could have come home to me?"

"'Twas to capture a traitor we knew was to be there this eve." His gaze softened. "I want no woman but you, Madalyn. Not now, and not ever."

"I love you, and you hurt me," she said quietly.

He stilled, her proclamation that she loved him sinking in and taking root. "I love you, too, Madalyn." His voice was pained, his expression tortured. "It nigh unto killed me, seeing you up on that stage. Unable to reveal myself to the enemy, I could do naught but watch whilst soldiers, warriors, and nobles alike coveted what is mine."

They stared at each other, adrenaline-induced by anger flaming into desire. Otar reached to her breasts and unclasped the bustier. It flew open, her breasts popping out.

"I'd kill any man who touched you," Otar ground out.

He palmed her breasts and rubbed her nipples. "You belong to me and only to me."

Madalyn moaned, the sensual massage making thought difficult. But something needed to be said. "The same for you, Otar. I can't stand the thought of you making another woman feel the way you make me feel."

His hands fell from her breasts and found the dragon. He unclasped it, and she stood before him naked. His fingers sifted through her golden-red triangle before rubbing her clit.

"Vow to me that you will never fuck another man." He backed her toward their bed, his voice guttural, like an animal's warning growl. "Vow it."

"I promise," Madalyn soothed.

His strong fingers clasped her buttocks and kneaded them. His breathing was heavy, his jaw tight.

"I don't want any man but you touching me, Otar."

Teeth setting, he whirled his wife around and bodily pressed her stomach toward the bed. He grabbed her hips and pulled them upward, preparing to penetrate her from behind.

The dominance in Otar's touch was unnerving; Madalyn had never felt the full brunt of his possessiveness before. Her husband was always so stoic—she had never seen him so seemingly out of control.

"I love you, Madalyn," he rasped, his hard cock poking against her entry. He released one of her hips and used his hand to guide him to her welcoming flesh. Positioned, his hand returned to her hip, locking her into a submissive pose. "Always."

Otar surged into her on a growl, fingers digging into the flesh of her hips. She gasped as he mounted her, his cock thick and filling.

"Oh God," Madalyn breathed out, her nipples jutting out as he began rocking inside of her. He stroked in and out, the sound of her flesh suctioning his back in with every out-stroke reaching her ears.

He took her harder, faster, moaning and groaning as he surged into her. Skin slapped against skin, the scent of their combined arousal perfuming the small hut.

"My pussy feels so good," he ground out, fucking her at a wicked pace. His fingers dug harder into her hips as he ruthlessly branded her with his cock. *"Madalyn."*

She moaned as he rode her, breasts jiggling beneath her. She arched her buttocks up higher in the air, allowing him to sink into her to the hilt.

Over and over he fucked her, hard, merciless strokes meant to conquer and claim. One of his hands dropped from her hips and found her clit, his callused fingers rubbing it at a brisk pace.

"Oh—God-oh-God-oh-God."

Madalyn came quickly and fiercely, her body shaking from the violence of her orgasm. She cried out his name as he continued to thrust in and out of her, fast, deep strokes that further aroused her.

"I'm coming," Otar said thickly, his body tensing over

hers. He kept up the brutal pace, sinking into her depths over and over, again and again and again.

"Madalyn!"

Her name came out as a roar, a bellowing sound that was at once forceful and loving. His body stiffened as he came, a gush of warm semen filling her insides.

Madalyn collapsed onto the bed on her belly. Otar soon followed beside her, so as not to hurt her with his massive weight.

It took her a long moment to find the energy to move, but she located enough to snuggle into her husband's powerful embrace. She slowly fell asleep, enveloped by a feeling of security and completion she'd never before known in a man's arms.

THEY SLEPT FOR BARELY HALF AN HOUR before Otar reached for Madalyn, rousing her. Sleepy, but fully aware of her husband's larger-than-life presence next to her on the bed, she immediately noted that his territorial mindset hadn't waned from their earlier lovemaking session. He was as aroused and forbidding as ever.

Madalyn slowly turned over on her side, facing Otar. His gaze was as vulnerable as it was possessive. He wanted to know that she viewed herself as more than a captive bride, as more than an Outsider woman who'd been forced into dwelling below the ground with him. Otar wanted the reassurance that she now saw herself as his wife.

She understood his fears, but didn't know how to calm

them. Only time and patience would demonstrate the depth of her love for him.

"I missed you so much when you were gone," Madalyn whispered. She smiled softly.

"Show me," Otar said hoarsely. He grabbed his stiff cock by the base and guided it toward her mouth. "Show me that you belong to me, Madalyn."

His demeanor was one of dominance, a man who needed proof in every way a woman could give it that he was wanted. Madalyn didn't hesitate long enough to blink. She opened her mouth and accepted his stiff cock inside.

Otar groaned as he slowly sank into her, his muscles tense. She sucked him hard on his outstroke, causing him to hiss.

"Play with my balls," he thickly demanded, picking up the pace of his thrusts. "Gods, Madalyn," he gritted out, "I love the way you suck my cock."

His words encouraged her to suck faster. She bobbed her head up and down underneath him, greedily sucking him off. Otar moaned as he rode her, pumping in and out from between her lips at a frenzied pace.

The sound of wet mouth meeting stiff flesh echoed in the hut. His balls tightened, and she knew he was getting ready to explode.

"Suck my cock harder," he growled, throwing his hips at her. She could see his jaw tighten. "Faster."

Madalyn moaned as she sucked him hard, her head moving impossibly faster. He slammed into her mouth once, twice, three times more, then plucked his cock from between her lips with a popping sound.

"I want to come in my pussy," Otar told her, his breathing labored. Beads of perspiration soaked his hairline. Throwing her legs over his shoulders, he gripped her thighs as he pressed the head of his cock against her moist entrance. "I love you, Madalyn." Otar sank into her on a growl, plunging into her flesh to the hilt.

Madalyn gasped, her head falling back on the animal furs. "I love you, too," she breathed out. "I'm sorry I was too scared to tell you that before you left."

Her confession that she'd loved him for weeks made him impossibly stiffer inside of her. Nostrils flaring, Otar rode her hard, her breasts jiggling beneath him with every thrust.

The sound of flesh sucking in rigid flesh heightened Madalyn's arousal. His fingers dug into her thighs as he took her hard and fast, making her moan and groan. A carnal knot of tension coalesced in her belly.

"I'm coming," Madalyn gasped, sensation rocking her. He rode her harder and faster and—

"Oh God."

The knot in her belly burst, the hardest orgasm of her life, the possessiveness in his lovemaking driving her wild.

"Mine," Otar said hoarsely. He rode her like an animal, guttural growls erupting from his throat. His jugular bulged, every muscle in his body straining. *"All mine."*

Otar came on a bellow, his cock jerking inside of her. Madalyn continued to throw her hips at him, knowing how much her husband loved it when she used her intimate muscles to milk him for every bit of cum he had to give.

"Madalyn," he said huskily, slowly winding down the pace. "I love you so much."

They collapsed in each other's arms and lay that way for long minutes, neither moving or speaking.

Then again—Madalyn smiled, snuggling closer to her husband—words weren't needed. They both knew how they felt about each other.

Madalyn Mae Simon Thordsson finally understood what it meant to love and be loved in return with equal passion. Shanty Row might be undesirable to the rest of Lokitown, but it was the best place in the world for her to be.

Chapter Thirty-five

One month later

The Revolution ended with Toki's death and the rebels' victory. Hope and jubilation swamped New Sweden the day that Lord Nikolas Ericsson was crowned the new jarl and festivities sprang up everywhere, a party atmosphere engulfing the colony.

Otar was reinstated as a noble and as the rightful heir to his father's estate. Leaving Shanty Row behind had been a bit sad for Madalyn, as her memories there were mostly good ones for her. The posh Thordsson longhouse, however, more than made up for it. Annikki had wept the moment she stepped foot inside the palatial house she'd spent most of her life in.

Annikki was doing well in other ways, too. She and

Vardo continued their game of dodge and pursuit, but with each passing day, the cat grew closer to catching his mouse. Madalyn couldn't wait for Vardo and Annikki to marry. Both of them wanted it and both of them deserved the happiness that would come from finally being together.

Agata was no longer lacking in suitors, nobles and warriors congregating daily for the chance to speak with her. All of them hoped Otar would put his twin sister up on the bride auction block soon, but Madalyn knew Otar wouldn't do so until Agata said she was ready.

There was one man in particular, a noble named Aleski Pontus, who was always finding a reason to visit the Thordssons. Madalyn realized he was hoping to catch a glimpse of Agata, who, for reasons unknown, avoided him like the plague. She found her sister-in-law's behavior strange. Especially considering the fact that Agata dearly loved Vardo, and Aleski was his son.

Drake and Iiro had worked things out, too. Iiro had been raised in status from soldier to warrior and was given a new, larger home. After Drake cleared the home of any signs of alien activity, she moved in.

Shanty Rowers were developing a higher status, as well. The alehouse had been converted into a theater and was expected to become one of Lokitown's hot spots. Madalyn, Annikki, Agata, and Vardo were slated for their opening-night performance in less than two weeks. Annikki could hardly contain her enthusiasm; Vardo just wanted his kiss.

Best of all, Madalyn's relationship with Otar grew deeper

every day. If someone had told her the day she'd been captured in Alaska that a time would come when she couldn't bear the thought of a life without Otar, she would have told them they were insane.

But that time had come. Otar was not only her husband, but her best friend as well. They had already accomplished things that it took most couples years to perfect, like finishing each other's sentences and understanding each other's personalities.

But then, they spent a lot of time together, both happier in the other's presence than they could ever be out of it. Now that Otar worked from home, instead of at the grindstone, there was more time to be near each other. A definite bonus to her husband's reclaimed heritage.

In the parlor, rehearsing her lines for the upcoming play, Madalyn stopped midline when she heard familiar baaing sounds, followed by the equally common sound of Otar bellowing. Victoria and Thor must have gotten out of their corral again. Otar hated it when that happened because they had a tendency to eat everything in sight.

"Victoria!" Otar barked, stomping into the parlor. "Get your wife and be gone anon."

Madalyn grinned at her husband. He had called Victoria Thor and Thor Victoria for the longest time. It took him three weeks to get their names right, but now he never messed them up.

"They ate another pair of my braes," Otar complained to Madalyn. He raised a callused hand to his forehead and sighed. It was apparent that drama ran in the family. "They conspire against me to drive me daft."

"Awww, poor baby." Madalyn chuckled. Her eyes danced as she wrapped her arms around his waist. "Would you like me to shoo them into their corral for you?"

"I can do it," he grumbled. "But I need a kiss, first."

That was just fine, because she needed one, too. A slow, lingering liplock later, neither of them could recall why Otar had come into the parlor to begin with.

"Are you happy, Madalyn?" Otar asked, hugging her close to him. "'Tis my greatest wish to make you the contentest wife in all the world."

She smiled against his chest. Madalyn found it adorable how such a big, formidable man needed emotional reassurance.

"Your wish has come true." She gave Otar a big squeeze. "I never thought I could be so incredibly happy."

"Do you miss your old life at all?"

Madalyn shook her head. "Not at all."

"Nay?"

"Nope. Not even a little bit."

It was the truth. Madalyn Mae Thordsson née Simon had become an actress under the misguided notion that fame and fortune would equal love and completion. While she would always be proud of her acting accomplishments, she didn't miss the world aboveground in the least.

Her heart just wasn't there. If she was honest with herself, her heart hadn't been there for several years before the fateful meeting with her husband.

"I love you, Otar," Madalyn whispered. "Thank you for being mine."

He'd spoken those words to Madalyn before, and his gentle gaze told her that fact hadn't been lost on him.

"I love you, too, Madalyn." He kissed the top of her head. "Are you about done rehearsing, so I can woo you into the bed furs?"

She grinned, teasingly thumping his chest. "Is that all you ever think about?"

Otar winked. "Aye."

Snorting and crunching sounds reached their ears. They turned their heads in unison to see Victoria and Thor chomping on another leather victim.

"Ah gods!" Otar said, exasperated. "I will not have a single pair of braes to my name, do they have their say about it."

Madalyn laughed. "Go corral them, handsome, and I'll meet you in our bedroom in five minutes."

Otar kissed her and then stomped off toward the goats. "Go!" he bellowed. "The deuce of you will drive me to drink before the day is over!"

Grinning, Madalyn watched the most wonderful man in the world chase down the two hungriest goats in the world. She sighed with contentment, thankful for life's twists.

The Alabama girl was no longer a part of the Barbie world, and there was nothing about her old, superficial life that she missed.

Well, except for those piña coladas.